Bar Sinister

A Spadena Street Mystery

Also by Marian Allen

Novels
SAGE Book 1: The Fall of Onagros
SAGE Book 2: Bargain With Fate
SAGE Book 3: Silver and Iron
Sideshow in the Center Ring
A Dead Guy at the Summerhouse
The Wolves of Port Novo
(Previously Published as Eel's Reverence)

Short Story Collections
Lonnie, Me and. . . .
Lonnie, Me and the Hound of Hell
Turtle Feathers
The King of Cherokee Creek
MA's Monthly Hot Flashes: 2002-2009
Other Earth, Other Stars
Shifty

Visit the author at
http://MarianAllen.com

Bar Sinister

A Spadena Street Mystery

Marian Allen

Per Bastet

Bar Sinister: A Spadena Street Mystery

Copyright © 2019 Marian Allen

Published by Per Bastet Publications LLC, P.O. Box 3023 Corydon, IN 47112

Cover art by Marian Allen

ISBN 978-1-942166-66-5

Bar Sinister

A Spadena Street Mystery

Chapter 1

District Attorney Jack Pitt woke early, as always. As always, he made no attempt to move quietly in deference to his sleeping wife. Then he remembered she was on another of her ever-more-frequent and ever-more-lengthy visits to her mother, and felt cheated.

He considered calling her, just to keep his hand in, but decided he couldn't be bothered.

As he pulled his long black hair back and fastened it into a ponytail, he imagined a typical morning conversation.

"Sloth is a sin," he might say, in his courtroom voice.

"I bow to the expert," Barb would probably say.

He walked out on the imaginary conversation, as he would have on a real one.

Pitt locked his front door, did a few warm-up stretches, and jogged toward the abrupt end of his career and his life.

The sun was still low when Pitt turned onto Haymarket Street. He was thinking of the several empty properties he'd bought on this all-but-abandoned relic of an old slaughterhouse industry. His ponytail bounced against his back as he huffed along, breath fogging in the early spring chill.

The streetlights hadn't gone out yet, and he passed from one pool of brightness to another. He'd make a killing on this street when the city's development groups got wind of the mayor's Renovate for the Arts incentives. One day, this crumbling corridor would be lined with expensive renters

Bar Sinister

Pitt had no idea what, exactly. Some artsy shit, he supposed. Barb dealt with all the artsy shit. But his investment here would pay off, and pay off nicely.

He was near one of his properties when the sound of an approaching car overrode his own rhythmic huffing.

The car accelerated, jumped the curb, and knocked him flying. He smashed through a plate-glass window, landing hard and sliding with the force of his momentum. He was surprised that it didn't hurt. That was nice.

A car door slammed. Footsteps. A pause, then closer footsteps.

He felt warm and cozy. He hoped the person coming toward him wouldn't want him to get up. He was so comfortable.

A foot prodded him. He opened his eyes. It was someone he knew. Smiling. That was nice. A smile was a nice thing to see, last thing before you go to sleep.

Chapter 2

At 1 Spadena Street, a woman, skin the color of mahogany, hair salt-and-pepper and tightly curled, worked at the stove.

Another woman, her loose brown curls only beginning to show a little gray, shuffled in wearing flannel pajamas with hipster penguins on them.

"Well, Juss! You finally up?" The woman at the stove turned two slabs of ham over in the skillet. "I thought I was gonna have to come put an ice cube down your back."

"It's 8:30, Mama D," Juss said, using the name she'd grown up calling Doris Winston and sometimes still called her. Juss scratched her head, disarranging her hair into less disorder. "That isn't late."

"I guess not, when you work from home." Doris pushed the ham aside and broke a couple of eggs into the sizzling pan.

Was that a dig? Doris had laughed when Juss had announced her decision to set up as a Life Coach, and Juss had never forgotten it.

"Anyway, I don't have any appointments today. I don't think I do. I better check."

"Breakfast is almost ready," Doris called to Juss' back.

In her office, Juss checked her appointment book and was disappointed to find the day blank.

Happy thought. She flipped open the yellow pages,

found a temporary agency, and ordered a secretary. *Happy, happy.*

Back in the kitchen, she set the table and poured coffee for them both. When she was sure Doris was settled comfortably, she sat at an adjacent side of the square kitchen table and put her olive hand into Doris' darker one.

Doris prayed for deliverance, especially from the Seven Deadly Sins. Juss had no difficulty understanding that Sloth was particularly in her mind.

"I'm upping my game," Juss said. "Kicking it up a notch."

"Does that mean calling Volunteer Hotline to see who needs workers?"

"No. It means I'm having a temp agency send me a secretary."

"A *secretary?*"

Juss let Doris chew that over, along with her ham.

The older woman nodded, and Juss sat back with a smile.

"It's a good idea, isn't it? All my files in order, everything on the computer, spreadsheets, billing."

Doris sipped her coffee and muttered, "Bidniss. Whoever thought?"

Juss waved both hands at the house around them. "Whoever thought *this?*"

"True that, Baby Girl. True that."

Chapter 3

Kerry knew it was a hoax, but he took the assignment anyway.

I mean, there's no way I could actually get to work there. Cement block or cubicles — that's my fate.

He parked his green VW on the street in front of the little Storybook Style castle that was 1 Spadena Street. He approached the house as slowly as he could, under the rose-covered arch and up the flagstone walk, savoring the colors and scents of the pocket-handkerchief flowered lawns to either side. The flagstone walk led around a cylindrical tower to a door with a lion's-head knocker. He rapped.

After a minute, the door opened and he faced a tall, dark, heavy-featured woman in casual clothes.

"Yes?" she said, eyes flickering over him and behind him. "We're as churched up as we're ever going to be, so don't start."

"What? Oh, no, no." Kerry peered over her shoulder at a coat rack, padded waiting-room chairs, side tables filled with magazines and a door not open enough for him to see beyond. "I got a call this morning from the Louisa Bradley Temporary Agency."

The woman cracked a smile and relaxed the door a little wider. "Ohhh. You're the secretary. Shows you I'm not as enlightened as I think I am. I thought you'd be a woman." She stepped aside, and Kerry had to restrain himself from pulling out his cell phone and calling his wife, Schatzi, to tell her where he was.

He began, "Are you—"

"No, not me. Come on in the kitchen and wait for her. Went to get my sinus medicine for me. If I don't have it, I sound like I'm talking Pig Latin without the Latin." The woman gave an impressive nasal display. "I'm Doris Winston."

A miniscule black-and-white television on a kitchen shelf was broadcasting the news about a hit-and-run on Haymarket Street.

Doris snapped it off. "If it bleeds, it leads," she said. "But you got to keep current. Can't sit back here in our little Paradise and pretend the world doesn't touch us, can we?"

He and Schatzi had been saying the same thing to each other the night before, so Kerry could honestly agree, as he accepted what turned out to be the best coffee he'd ever tasted. The mini-muffins were darned good, too, but loyalty made him give Schatzi's the edge over them.

He moved the sugar bowl and cream pitcher, each shaped like a blue-and-white Delft cow, into adjacent positions in the center of the table and asked, "Can you tell me what I'll be doing?"

Doris sat across from him, large, wide-set brown eyes focused on him with disturbing intensity.

"Computery things, I gather. Juss is a Life Coach. That's yuppie talk for 'I can't think for myself and I won't listen to my mother.'"

Kerry was thinking, *Must pay pretty well,* when Doris said,

"Her grandmom left some money and she quit her real job, to leave it for somebody who needed it. Bagging groceries. At her age, and with a college degree."

Doris shook her head, not looking at Kerry. He had the impression she was seeing something else — maybe the past, maybe his temporary employer — and that what she saw made her so sad it was overflowing into words to a stranger.

Kerry hadn't been about to ask, but Doris said, "I'm retired. Twenty-five years in furniture sales, ten of them in management. Oakland Brothers."

A little above his and Schatzi's budget, but he knew the store. He realized he hadn't introduced himself, but it would seem awkward at this late juncture, and he always avoided it, if he could.

Chapter 4

Juss pulled into the garage, grabbed her bags and went through into the house. She wondered if she should check the waiting room first, in case the green VW out front belonged to a walk-in client, but she heard voices from the kitchen.

A man, sharing coffee and mini-muffins with Doris, rose at her entrance. A pretty darned good-looking man.

Taller than her own 5-7, peaches-and-cream complexion, light brown hair, dark brown eyes, Clark Gable mustache, and his slight pudginess didn't even begin to spoil the scenery.

"Hi, there," she said.

Doris said, "This is your secretary."

Juss picked up the rectangle of flimsies on the corner of the table.

Doris stood and carried her own plate and mug to the sink. "I better get back to work. You two introduce yourselves."

Juss handed over a small bag. "Your meds." She stuck the other bag, white paper, into the refrigerator. "And I stopped by Melton's and got a ham hock."

"Mmmm. Split pea soup!" With a bright grin, Doris left the room.

Juss looked at the flimsies, a time sheet for K. W. Dashingly.

"Dashingly? Your name is Dashingly? For real?"

"Yes," he said dryly, stroking his mustache. "Why? Is it funny?"

"Not as funny as mine." Juss held out her hand. "I'm Injustice H. Chocolate, believe it or not. The "H" stands for Harbridge, so it's not like I could use my middle name, either. Most folks call me Juss, rhymes with cuss."

He took her hand and they shook solemnly, fellow-sufferers, friends for life. "I'm Kerry." He hesitated, then said, "Kermit Watchman Dashingly."

"You poor bastard," said Juss. "Were your parents hippies, too?"

He laughed. "Far from it. Kermit and Watchman are old family names. So is Dashingly, come to that."

"All of mine are made up, which shows you what kind of people my parents were. Or are, as the case may be." Before he could ask her what that meant, she said, "Anyway, you're a secretary, right?"

"Office worker in general. I can take shorthand. I'm familiar with computers. I can set up and deal with databases. I can set up and use simple spreadsheets." He opened empty hands. "Your . . . uh . . . Doris didn't seem to know exactly what you hired me to do."

She waved a hand. "Keep track of appointments for me, do letters, that kind of thing. I'm a Life Coach. Doris says it's the perfect job for busybodies." She grinned. "That's me. Come on, I'll show you around."

Chapter 5

Kerry wasn't sure he liked his new employer. She had a long sharp nose; when she smiled and her upper lip came down to a point in the middle, she looked like a good-natured emu. But an emu. They bit, he had been told.

"Doris raised me," Juss said, opening a door at the end of the short hall. "Waiting room. I guess you came through it, unless you went around back." She opened a door to the right. "Living room and library."

Bookcases lined the walls, floor to ceiling, even surrounding the picture window and fireplace. "Doris and I like books."

"So do I." Kerry inhaled the scent of leather and paper and caught no trace of must. The books were well-kept, not shelved and left to moulder.

"Is this where I'll be working?"

"No, you'll be in the office. I'll get you a desk."

"Your regular secretary doesn't have a desk?"

"I don't have a regular secretary. I feel my business has now reached the point at which I require secretarial help."

That was when Kerry realized she had called without really having anything for a secretary to do. *So much for this assignment.* It wouldn't be the first temp job that had turned out to be more temporary than expected, but he loved being on Spadena Street, even for a day. He loved the thought of working in a tiny castle, and he loved this library.

Juss rubbed her hands together as if getting down to brass tacks. "First order of business: buy a desk and stuff."

He hated to say it, but he felt obligated to. "Why buy office furniture when you don't really know if you'll need a permanent secretary?"

She started to look like she was thinking about biting. "Office furniture doesn't eat. It won't hurt to have it, and there's plenty of room. And I think I *do* need a secretary."

"You know best," Kerry said, with what he hoped was an emu-friendly smile. Inspiration struck. "Have you had the books cataloged? Have they been valued?"

"Probably. Maybe. I don't know. Great-grandmama probably had it done." She looked around, as if a catalog would push itself out of one of the shelves and wave to her.

"I was trained in library science."

"You were? I always thought librarians had tight little buns—"

Juss stopped with her mouth open and flushed to her hairline.

Schatzi will love that one. Kerry smiled. "I know what you meant."

She walked out of the room, not looking at him when she passed, and opened the door on the left. "Here's the office."

He followed her in.

Doris looked up from the far window and waved her feather duster.

Juss said, "Hey, Doris. Showing the new guy around." To Kerry, she said, "You can see, there's plenty of room for both of us."

There certainly was. The kidney-shaped desk in front of the window looked lonely in the big room, even with a comfy chair and a side table in front of it.

Doris said, "Your poor little lost lambs won't like airing their lazy troubles in front of a witness."

"They're not lazy!"

Kerry disapproved of people in authority speaking harshly to their employees, but he rather admired Juss for standing up for her clients.

Then she said, "Well, some of them are lazy, but some of them are all tangled up inside. Not everybody has a Mama D, Mama D."

Doris dusted Juss' face.

"Doris has a point, though," Kerry said. He wasn't a natural eavesdropper, but he didn't trust himself not to strain to pick up interesting tidbits to share with Schatzi. "Perhaps, given my task, it would be more efficient for me to headquarter in the library."

"Kerry's going to catalog the books and get them evaluated."

"Your great-grandma did that."

"For her books. Not for Great-grandpapa's. And there's Granny Ruth and Grandpa's and yours and mine."

"I don't think ours—"

Eight bars of "Who Wrote the Book of Love?" toodled from Kerry's inside jacket pocket.

"I beg your pardon. I should have put it on vibrate." He checked the phone but, before he could turn off the ringer, Juss spoke.

"Go on and take it, if you need to. Go ahead. It might be an emergency."

"It's my cousin Abigail," he said. "It's always an

emergency with Abby."

"Take it, then. Go on."

Kerry had the feeling he was in the presence of the queen of all natural eavesdroppers. *Busybody*, she had called herself. *Ah, well.*

Abby's high-pitched panic squawk split the air as Kerry held the phone away from his ear.

"Kerry, he's dead! Jack Pitt! Hit and run this morning! Oh, God, what if they think I did it?"

Jack Pitt! His first thought was *Good Riddance.* Then shame slapped his conscience awake and he understood why Abby was upset. "Calm down," he said. "Why would they?"

"I don't want to be alone. What if they come to question me? Can you come over?"

"I'm at work now. Go to that coffee shop you like and have a cup. Decaf. I'll call you on my lunch break."

"What if they come there? What if I get scared at the coffee shop? Can I call you from there if I need to, Kerry? Can I?"

"Yes, of course you can. Or call Schatzi, if you need to talk to somebody. Calm down; it'll be all right. Everything will be all right. Okay?"

After a few more sobs that wrenched his heart, she sniffled and whispered, "Okay."

"Sounds like trouble." Juss cocked her head to the side and fixed Kerry with one big emu eye. "Let's go desk shopping and you can tell me about it."

"Here we go," said Doris.

Chapter 6

Juss led the way through the kitchen to the attached garage. Doris's big blue Buick needed washing. Maybe she'd do that this afternoon, if it was sunny.

I can't wash the car with a secretary around. Maybe I can send him home early. She tried not to frown. *See, it's true: Less is more. You hire a secretary, and you make limits for yourself.*

She unlocked her own pristine little black-and-white Morris Mini-Cooper and slid into the driver's seat. She reached for the sun visor and stopped.

I can't wear my hat in front of a secretary. She silently growled at herself. *I can, too! Who's the boss around here, anyway?*

She slid a Colts ball cap from under the visor and tugged it on defiantly.

"Oh, the Colts," Kerry said as he buckled his seat belt. "Schatzi and I always root for them. It's more fun when you root for somebody, isn't it?"

"Exactly!" Maybe this secretary thing would be okay, after all. Maybe he was sympatico, and not all judgy like he looked, with his pencil-thin mustache and his nice hair and his suit and tie.

She eased from the driveway into the street, acutely conscious that everybody in the two-block neighborhood knew she was leaving and had a man in the car. Doris would have been able to name the ones out walking and give their life stories and tell who each one would go inside

14

and phone to say, "Guess who drove out with a man in her car? No, I don't know who he is. He must have come in that green VW at the curb in front."

Oh, hell, there goes one up to the house. Clever! While lesser gossips were spreading speculation, she was busy getting the goods from Doris. *Well, let 'em know I've got a secretary! A boy one! See what they make out of that!*

"I love your neighborhood," Kerry said. "Schatzi and I come here to view the decorations at Christmas. Schatzi tells me the architecture of all these different looks is called Storybook Style. But I suppose you know that."

"I didn't. But it makes sense. Storybook. Yeah, Christmas looks like Disney on crack."

Kerry gave a surprised little yip of laughter. "Don't you love it?"

"I do, actually." She was surprised to hear herself say it, and even more surprised that she felt it. *It isn't the neighborhood's fault*, she admonished herself. *What isn't the neighborhood's fault? Nothing. None of it.*

She flipped on the local news. "I need to keep current," she said. "For my clients."

It was the top of the hour, and the news brief featured the death of Jack Pitt.

"Oh, my," said Kerry, turning toward the radio as if that would help him hear it better.

Pitt had been stuck by a car during his morning jog and knocked through a glass window. Death had not been instantaneous, but he had been dead by the time his body was found. There would be an autopsy. All the stops would be pulled out to find the driver of the vehicle. The driver was being appealed to — accidents happened, and leaving the scene of an accident was a crime, but it would be less serious if owned up to. Could it have been a deliberate homicide? No comment. Jack Pitt left a widow, the former Barbara Lanski, and a daughter, Sharon Pitt, by his deceased ex-wife, Laureen Breeden Pitt. None of the women could be reached for comment.

The show after the headline news was a local talk hour, and the first segment was on the death and the victim. It would have made a good drinking game to down a shot every time one of the participants prefaced a remark by saying, "Not to speak ill of the dead, but. . . ."

"He sounds like kind of a stinker," she told Kerry.

"Naturally, *I* have no use for him."

"What'd he do to you?"

"Not me, my cousin. The one who called. This is what she was so upset about. She's afraid she'll be arrested for the murder."

"Hoo! What did she do, make a death threat?"

"No. She's just spooked. That's just Abby." He sighed. "She's a little bit flighty — well, no, that sounds like too much fun for Abby. She's easily distracted. So her insurance lapsed. Then a woman ran into her and accused *Abby* of reckless driving, and Abby was uninsured, which is an automatic guilty in this state, besides being illegal."

Juss turned into Boswick's parking lot. She found a space not much bigger than a motorcycle, but one of the joys of driving a Mini-Cooper was being able to use a doghouse as a parking garage. *Happy.*

Kerry hopped out and opened Juss' door for her.

He'd look cute in one of those chauffeur's uniforms with a little cap and all.

Juss shook her head to get that flea out of her ear and said, "Thanks." She locked the door and returned to the topic at hand. "Doesn't that usually pull a fine and maybe driving school? What does Pitt have to do with it?"

"He prosecuted her for it. Took her to criminal court. Abby is very shy, rather highly strung. It was quite difficult for her."

"She do time?"

"Oh, good Lord, no. I don't believe she would have survived that shock."

Abby sounded too precious for this earth. Even most of Juss' Life Coach clients were rugged free-thinkers compared to Little Miss Uninsured Motorist.

Kerry opened the door to Boswick's for her and they stepped into office heaven.

She would get something really nice; it would be beautiful furniture, besides being functional. She resented putting so much money in a manufacturer's pocket, but it would help pay the workers' salaries, too, and it would give a salesperson a nice fat commission.

A customer service representative, recognizing Juss from previous visits, put on some speed and hustled over to her.

"Wonderful to see you again!" he said, and he meant it.

Chapter 7

Abby did feel better when she got to CT 'Scape. The quiet bustle of people minding their own business was soothing. It was kind of like being in an apartment building with invisible walls. She was conscious of life and activity all around her, but she wasn't required to deal with it. She wasn't alone, but she was private.

And Beej was behind the counter. She pushed her mousy brown frizz off her forehead and smiled.

Beej looked at her with those big chocolate eyes over those strong cheekbones and smiled back. He was engaged to a girl from the old country — Azerbaijan or somewhere, so his friendliness wasn't threatening. Abby could enjoy it without getting her hopes up or worrying about her life getting more stressed than it already was.

"Hey, Abby! Early for you, isn't it? I had to pick up a morning shift; thought I wouldn't get to see my biscotti buddy today. You want the usual?"

"Um, no. I want the house decaf today."

"Medium in a large cup, to make room for the fixin's."

"Um, yes."

"Biscotti, yes? What flavor today?"

"Um, surprise me."

"Surprise me, it is. Get your car fixed yet?"

She shook her head.

Beej leaned forward and muttered, "Insured yet?"

Abby blushed and nodded.

He patted her hand. "Good girl. Hey, if the car runs, it's all good, yes?" He pushed a cup across the counter and handed her a cellophane-wrapped packet. "One house decaf with plenty of room and one 'surprise me' biscotti."

Abby took her order to the extras counter and loaded her cup with sugar and half-and-half, found an empty table, and sat down by one of the windows. She wished she had thought to bring a book, but she liked people-watching, too. She stirred her coffee enough to dissolve some of the sugar but still to leave a good dose of it on the bottom, so her last gulp would be like a mouthful of coffee-flavored candy.

The accident. She didn't want to think about the accident. The shock of the impact, of her car rocking and skidding sideways; the faces of the people in the traffic lane, most of them moving on as soon as they could; the woman who had plowed into her, screaming accusations; the policeman comforting the small, pretty, hysterical babe in the expensive auto and turning a blank stare on the gawky, plain, stunned woman in the rattletrap with so many old dents, the fresh ones hardly mattered. Then finding the envelope with the check to the insurance company's final notice still in her purse. Uninsured. Her stomach twisted again.

And now Jack Pitt was dead. Her hatred for him was so ingrained, it was hard to summon up any other emotion, but fear made a breakthrough. Everybody knew she hated him. She had made no secret about that. And now he was dead. They would be looking at everybody who had a motive, and hatred was surely a motive for murder. If they suspected her, they would come after her, and they would get her. That was the kind of person she was — the kind who took the fall for everything. When the girls beside her in elementary school had been talking, *she'd* gotten in trouble for it.

She reached for her cell phone with trembling hands. Kerry was at work. Schatzi was probably doing something.

The chair across from her slid out, and Beej sat down, a cup of what smelled like chai and a biscotti in his hands.

"Hey, buddy!" he said.

Abby let go of her cell and relaxed.

~*~

By the time she got home, her coffee house interlude had calmed her nerves. Still, she avoided the television and radio while she had a microwave lunch, and didn't fire up her computer to check the local headlines or browse social media.

Library. I need to take my books back. I'll get something nice. Something about horses or non-fiction about handicrafts. Maybe I'll take up scrapbooking.

She gathered her books. *The Art of Maxfield Parrish* was missing. *Did I take that one back already? I think I did. Did I remember to put it in the book slot? I didn't see it next to me on the way to the coffee house. Maybe it's in the back seat.*

She zipped her books into her Hello Kitty backpack and scuttled downstairs.

She felt a pang, as always, looking at the ruins of her rear passenger side door, the broken window still "replaced" by cardboard and duct tape. She felt again the impact as the other car dodged out of traffic and into her, inconveniently in the way and absentmindedly uninsured.

At least the door still worked. She unlocked the car and winced at the opening screech.

With a shriek of her own, she jumped back and slammed the door.

A bass voice asked, "Something wrong?"

Abby spun around. A skinny young policeman wheeled his official bicycle from behind the neighbors' white van.

"A rat!" Abby barely gasped the words out. "There's a rat in my car! A big black rat! Get it out!" She gave the policeman an apologetic look. "Um, please?"

"What's your name, Miss?"

"Um, Abby. Abigail Andrews."

"Is this your vehicle, Miss Andrews?"

"Um, yes. Yes, sir."

"Are you asking me to open your car, Miss Andrews?"

"Yes, please."

"If I find something, what do you want me to do with it?"

"Um, get it out? Please?"

"Happy to oblige."

"Thank you! I'll go. . . ." She scurried onto the porch, holding Hello Kitty in front of her for protection from all rodents.

He pulled a small digital camera out of one of his pockets, his hands surprisingly dexterous in their thin black cycling gloves. He snapped a picture of the car, then a closer picture of the door.

"W-why are you doing that?"

"For the record."

"What record?"

He opened the car and snapped the interior, then the floor. He closed the door, raised a hand to the radio on his shoulder and smiled sympathetically at Abby's wide-eyed face.

"I need to call someone, now. Maybe you need to call someone, too."

Chapter 8

Kerry hadn't dreamed that office furniture could be so expensive. He tentatively pointed out some pieces that were more modest, but Juss patted his arm and let the salesman show her solid cherry desks with hand-carved detail, ergonomic chairs, desk sets covered in Florentine gilded leather, and super-speed desktop computers with all the trimmings, including office programs he'd only heard about.

She consulted him on those, and he ventured to recommend one his library science professor had raved about. "We'll have that one," she said, waving away his objection to the price.

She sang on the way home. "*I got a desk, you got a desk, all God's children got desks. When I get to heaven, gonna sit at my desk, gonna work all over God's heaven.*"

It was like a game he and Schatzi might play with the kids on vacation. When she finished the chorus, Kerry did a verse.

"*I got a chair, you got a chair, all God's children got chairs. When I get to heaven, gonna sit on my chair, gonna roll all over God's heaven.*"

Juss delighted him by breaking into a multi-layered chest-and-belly laugh, the laugh of a baby playing peek-a-boo.

Oh! I'm going to have so much to tell Schatzi!

Her good mood faded as they turned onto Spadena Street, and she tugged her ball cap lower.

One of the neighbors was watering her lawn and waved the hose at them as they passed. Kerry, charmed, waved back.

"Don't wave," Juss growled. "It'll only encourage them."

"Encourage them to what?"

"Pry."

"Do they pry?"

She made a scornful sound. "You saw the one going in the house as we left. I'm not a reality show. My business is none of theirs."

She looked ready to bite, so Kerry kept quiet.

When they got into the utility room, she said, "I'm going up the back stairs. If the tourist is gone, tell Doris to let me know."

He went through into the kitchen, where Doris was stirring a pot of soup.

"Juss went up the back stairs. She said to tell her if the tourist is gone."

Doris shook her head and pressed a button next to a grid in the wall.

"They're not tourists, Girl Child. The word is 'neighbors.' Your new secretary can spell that for you."

Juss' voice came through very small and thin: "I'll be down in a minute."

"She's a people junkie," Doris told Kerry. "Has to have 'em. Just wants to go fetch 'em herself." She shrugged. "Could be worse, I guess."

Kerry fidgeted with the change in his pocket, then reminded himself not to. Were he and this woman fellow employees, or was he lower in status because he was new, or what? Would it be rude to be personal, or rude not to?

He settled on semi-personal. "She said you raised her."

Doris tasted the soup with a teaspoon, nodded at it, then nodded at Kerry. "Lots of us raised her. Her mama and daddy and a bunch of other ones and I were in this little commune on a farm near here."

He remembered Juss' asking him if his parents were hippies, too. Now, the question made sense.

Doris said, "This was in the '60s-'70s. We all took care of all the young ones, but some of the mamas felt like their kids weren't getting the best. Supposed to be share and share alike, but mamas kind of get selfish for their kids, sometimes. I don't fault them for that."

Doris began taking dishes and flatware out and setting piles on the table.

"May I help?"

"Well, thank y'sir."

Kerry got the feeling that Doris' "sir" wasn't a mockery, but it wasn't subservience, either. It was like a joke between friends, and the knowledge that his position was only temporary gave him a pang of pre-nostalgia.

Juss stuck her head in the door and said, "I'm going to check my email while my porridge cools."

"We eat together in this house," Doris said.

"Yes, ma'am, Mama D, but everybody's porridge is too hot."

"Go ahead, then, Goldilocks, but don't be long." She asked Kerry, "You mind? I can put your soup back and keep it hot."

He placed the last spoon and adjusted it satisfactorily. "No, thanks; hot porridge hurts my fillings."

"You're a nice man."

Kerry, startled, couldn't think of anything to say for a moment, then managed, "Thank you."

"You're welcome. Sweet tea or water?"

"Tea, please."

"It's *sweet*. How we like it."

"I like my cold tea sweet."

"Anyway," Doris lowered her voice to be sure Juss wouldn't catch what she said, "Juss loved growing up there. Loved being a part of everybody's business. She never cared if she had the biggest piece or the most or the first or even anything, as long as she could be there when whatever it was happened. Shared or gave away anything she did get, like it was human nature."

She got out an ice bin and started filling tall glasses with cubes. As she filled one, Kerry took it to the table and put it carefully in a precise spot, at an angle and a distance from a plate precisely the same as every other glass's position from its plate.

Doris, slowing on filling the last glass in order to watch him, said, "Only thing she didn't like was when folks from around and about would come out on a day trip to see how we lived. Some of them loved to try to get one of the children aside and pump them for information. You know, 'How many daddies do you have?' 'Where does everybody sleep?' That kind of thing."

"That explains her objection to 'tourists'," Kerry said.

Doris waved that away with a pitcher of tea and filled the glasses. "You're not just supposed to get older; you're supposed to grow up. Not everybody who wants to know your business wants to make fun of it. She, of *all* people, ought to know that."

That seemed a fair claim against a Life Coach.

Doris sat down and motioned for Kerry to sit, too. Apparently, they didn't have to wait until they were all at the table to drink their tea.

She said, "The other mamas and daddies took their children and left, and *her* mama and daddy just left."

A chill stiffened the skin on the back of Kerry's head. He had children. He couldn't have heard right. "They left? Left her?"

She nodded and sipped her tea, eyes in the past. "Told me to take care of her till they got back, and that was the last any of us heard of them. When she was about ten, the few of us that were still there at the commune decided to quit — too much work, not enough hands — and I brought her here to her Granny Ruth, her daddy's mother. Granny Ruth took her to see Juss' daddy's grandma, who was rich. That one had cut Juss's daddy out of her will when he went off to be a hippie. She wouldn't have anything to do with Juss; wouldn't even see her except that once. Little bitty helpless thing, wasn't but ten years old, and this old battleaxe looked down her nose at her and insulted the child's momma and daddy. Juss called her a 'running-dog flunky of the Capitalist/Industrialist system' — "

She had to stop while Kerry struggled successfully not to spit his tea across the table, then went on, still keeping her voice down and her eye on the door.

"Juss' great-grandma owned this house, and only let Grannie Ruth live here, and she flat-out forbade Juss from living here, too. So I got a job and an apartment and kept right on looking after the child like always. It would have killed me not to. By that time, she was *mine*."

He hoped she would tell him how Juss had gone from forbbiden-to-live-here to owner, but she didn't have time.

27

The strains of "I'm an old cowhand from the Rio Grande" sounded from the hall, with the words changed to, "I'm a Google queen and you're on my screen." Juss came in, looking, Kerry thought, like a very smug emu, indeed.

"While I was at it," she said, "I Googled Jack Pitt. There've been complaints about him to the Bar Association and the HR departments at the courthouse and his law firm. Not a nice man. That makes for plenty of suspects. I don't think your cousin has anything to worry about."

Kerry had never supposed she did, but it might ease Abby's mind for him to tell her a Life Coach thought the same.

Juss sat down and held out her hands. Doris took one and reached across the table to Kerry. Kerry understood, and took the offered hands and bowed his head.

"You do the honors, Girl Child," Doris said.

"God or Goddess, the universe or chance, we're thankful for this bounty."

"Amen," Doris said.

Chapter 9

They were nearly finished when Kerry jumped.

"What is it?" Juss asked.

"Hiccups," Doris said.

Kerry put a hand on his quivering jacket pocket. "No, I set my phone on vibrate, and it did. It is. It startled me."

"Answer it," Juss urged.

"No, I don't like to, at the table."

"The man has manners," Doris said.

"Go on, it's probably Abby. You could set her mind at rest."

"Excuse me, then." He took the phone out as he left the room.

As soon as he answered, hysterical squeaks and squawks sent static into his ear.

"Abby, I can't understand you. I can't understand you! Calm down, sweetheart. I'm listening to you, but you need to calm down a little. Just a little, Abby. Breathe."

Abby stopped talking and drew deep breaths that she let out in sobs. Kerry waited impatiently, knowing he couldn't give her Juss' reassurance until she vented her own fear a little.

Finally, she could speak coherently, and Juss' comfort evaporated before he could share it.

"Oh, Kerry! I went out to the car and there was something in it and there was a policeman and I asked him to get it out and he opened the car and there was something there and he called some other policemen and he told me to call somebody. Kerry, I'm scared."

"What was in the car?"

"I don't know! A rat, I thought. I don't know, but I'm scared! He told me to call somebody and I didn't know who else to call. I'm sorry." She collapsed into gulping sobs.

"I'll— " He looked back into the kitchen. Doris was courteously pretending not to listen, but Juss was riveted, her big brown eyes shining. He went into the office and closed the door. "Do you have a lawyer?"

Abby tried to talk. He couldn't understand the words, but it was pretty clear that the answer was no.

"Schatzi and I updated our wills last year, but we went to a civil lawyer. Sounds like you need a criminal lawyer."

"Oh, Kerry! Oh, oh, oh! Please help me!"

"All right, sweetheart, calm down." He patted the air as if he had her shoulder in reach. He turned the phone away from his mouth and puffed a sigh, then brought the mouthpiece back. "Look, I'm at work, but I'm not really needed. I'll tell my employer to clock me out and I'll be right over. If. . . . If you have to leave— " It was the least threatening way he could put the possibility of her arrest. "If you have to leave, write me a note and stick it under the mat. The one in front of your apartment door, not the one in front of the building door. Okay? Okay?"

"Okay."

"Abby, what will you do if you have to leave?"

"Um, uh, write a note and leave it under the apartment mat."

"Good girl. I'll be there as soon as I can."

"Stay on the phone with me?"

Oh, Lord.

30

"Abby, I— "

"Please?"

He suppressed another sigh, but Abby was clearly on the verge of lunacy, so he agreed. He switched to his hands-free Starship Enterprise ear phone and put the handset away, heading back to the kitchen.

"I'm still here," he told his cousin as he walked. "All right?"

"All right." Abby seemed marginally calmer. "Kerry, maybe it *was* a rat. Maybe there's a plague they aren't telling us about."

"Hold that good thought, Abby. I need to talk to my employer now."

"Trouble?" Juss asked — hopefully, he thought — as he came in.

"Abby ran afoul of the law again. She doesn't know what it is, but a policeman found something in her car. She needs me to come over and help her find a lawyer."

Juss put her napkin on the table. "*We* have a lawyer."

"She needs a criminal lawyer, I think."

"DW can do anything. I'll call him," Juss said, loud enough for Abby to hear. "We'll be right over."

"I stay out of other people's business," Doris said, then she granted Juss a small, approving smile. "But these folks need help. Go on, Injustice H. Chocolate, Life Coach. Rah, rah."

Chapter 10

The young cop stayed near the car, but turned his back, giving Abby what privacy he could. He got his bike and moved it up onto the verge, leaning it against a big sycamore, out of the street and off of the sidewalk.

Abby watched him rise onto his toes, hold that position, then lower himself. She found herself mentally counting, "And UP two three and DOWN two three." It did more to calm her than the always-reassuring tone of Kerry's voice over the phone. She could hear a woman's voice in the background. *Kerry's new boss? Why is she coming with him?*

She suddenly realized the young policeman really *was* doing exercises. Making good use of the time. Admirable.

"Kerry. . . . Kerry, the police are here. I mean, the other police. Whoever he called. I can see the cruiser coming."

"Look the other way," he said.

What good would it do to turn away? In response to his repetition of the order, she faced the other direction. "Oh, yes, I see your car! Oh, good!"

She ended the call and dropped her phone into the bottomless depths of her backpack.

While Kerry parked, she looked back at the cruiser. It stopped, blocking her driveway. The young officer motioned for her to stay on the porch while he went to meet the brown car with the star on the door.

Both doors opened. A woman got out of the passenger side.

Abby knew her: "Scout" Young, the Chief Deputy Sheriff. Whatever the young cop had found must be important, to bring her out. Everybody knew Scout was the paperwork queen, the administration part of the Sheriff's Office. Maybe she had come out to keep in practice. Or maybe somebody called in sick and she was filling in.

Scout glanced at her, and Abby raised a hand in a weak wave. Scout didn't wave back, concentrating on what she was being told. The young man led her up the drive to Abby's car and opened the door. She squatted to get a better look at the rat or whatever it was and nodded as he talked.

Abby shifted from foot to foot, willing Kerry to hurry. She was beginning to feel light-headed.

A deep blue Mercedes drove past and parked. The door opened just as the driver's door of the Sheriff's Department cruiser swung wide, and bookend men stepped out, huge and black from the Mercedes, huge and white from the cruiser.

She knew the white one. *Carlton Cornflower!* Abby had never met the Sheriff, but she had seen him around town, naturally, and his picture was in the local paper often enough. His time-yellowed once-red hair bristled in a flat-top haircut, and his pale green eyes always seemed to be x-raying your most casual statements for untruth particles. Any hope that what she had found was not really that important died a quiet death. The Sheriff and the Chief Deputy. She leaned against a porch post and slid down to sit on the top step.

Sheriff Cornflower and the big black man met in the middle of the street and shook hands, clapping each other on the shoulder, obviously old friends.

Kerry and the woman Abby assumed was his boss joined the two big men and exchanged introductions. Scout stood up, but waited for the group to join her, blocking their view of the back seat and whatever was in it. Cornflower pointed to the porch. The woman with Kerry hung back, craning her neck, but the big black man wrapped a hand around her upper arm and drew her along.

"It's all right, Abby," Kerry called.

The woman's attention swung around, and now the big man was holding her back.

Abby pulled herself to her feet and let Kerry's embrace keep her from collapsing.

"Now, now," he said, patting her the way her mother had, before Momma had remarried and moved all the way to Arizona. "It's all right, Abby," Kerry said. "It's all right. Come on. I want you to meet some people."

He helped her down the steps to where the woman waited, eyes shining, broad smile on her face, hand extended.

"Abigail Andrews, this is my current employer, Juss Chocolate."

"Excuse me?" *I must have heard wrong.*

"Chocolate," the woman said. "Injustice H. Chocolate. Once you hear the 'Injustice' part, the 'Chocolate' part doesn't sound so bad, does it? Call me Juss."

Abby shook her hand. "I'm Abby."

"And this is your lawyer, Dexter Walter Delaney."

The lawyer tugged at the brim of his soft hat and said, "Miss Andrews. Don't let Miss Chocolate rush you into anything. I'm your lawyer, *if you want me.*"

"Yes," Abby said with what breath she could push out.

34

"Please. Thank you." She held out a hand and Mr. Delaney shook it with the gravity of signing a contract.

"Try to relax," he said. "I know how anxious you must be."

Oddly, his acknowledgement loosened the band of fear that was choking her.

"What—" Juss began, but Mr. Delaney raised a hand and she stopped.

"Have you been questioned yet?"

"Um . . . no."

"Good. Tell me what happened."

So much, for so long. "When?"

"Let's start with this morning. Let's start with what the police already know."

"Um . . . well, I came out and I opened the back door of the car and I saw a thing on the floor and I thought it was a rat and I jumped back," she took a breath, "and then I saw the policeman and I asked him to help me and he opened the door," another breath, "and he started taking pictures and then he called somebody on his shoulder thing and he thought I ought to call somebody, too."

"Did you see the policeman before you opened the door?"

"No, he came up after I screamed. He had a bike."

"He rode up on the bike, or he came up on foot?"

"Um . . . on foot. Yes, his bike was parked in the street."

"Did you go anywhere before you came out and saw the thing and the policeman came up?"

"Um . . . to the CT 'Scape. It's a coffee house."

"Did you drive?"

"Um . . . yes."

"Did you look in the back at that time?"

"Um . . . no. I didn't need to. I looked in the back this time because I thought I might have left a library book back there."

"What time did you go?"

"To the library?"

"To the coffee house."

"Um . . . Right after I called Kerry. Kerry, what time did I call you?"

Kerry checked his cell phone. "10:17."

"We talked a couple of minutes, and then I left a few minutes after that."

"And you didn't go out before that?"

"Um . . . no."

"Do you keep your car locked?"

"Um . . . yes."

"Invariably?"

Abby's eyes widened until Juss was afraid they'd fall out.

Juss had a client who was trying to live without medication, but worried constantly if she had locked the door, locked the car, turned off the oven/iron/whatever. Abby probably checked compulsively, but was never securely certain.

Abby said, "I . . . I *think* so."

"All right. Any questions that involve those facts and any general questions — your name and address and so on, answer as briefly as possible and, of course, as honestly. Anything else, look at me and I'll nod for yes or shake my head for no. Understood?"

She nodded, pressing a hand to her chest, where her heart pounded so hard she could feel the pulse throbbing in her temples.

Abby saw movement beyond Mr. Delaney's arm and scooted back until her heels hit the bottom step of the porch. The police were coming toward her.

Mr. Delaney and Kerry and his boss — Juss — turned to face them, and the light-headedness drained away. She felt championed.

The young policeman — Abby had read his name tag: Alan Cunningham — said, "Miss Andrews, this here is the Sheriff, Carlton Cornflower, and the Chief Deputy, Jean Louise Young."

"Hello," Abby said faintly.

"DW," Scout said.

"Jean Louise. What brings you out into the mean streets of Jorisburg?"

The sheriff answered, "We need to question this woman, DW. Is that going to be a problem?"

"Not at all," Mr. Delaney said. "Will this be lengthy?"

"Don't know yet, 'til we see what some of the answers are." The sheriff took out a notebook and flipped it open. He clicked a ballpoint pen and wrote at the top of the page.

What's he writing? He hasn't asked me anything yet.

"What's your full name, Miss?"

"Abigail Anne Andrews. Anne with an e. On the end."

"Yes, ma'am. Address?"

"910 Yancy Street, Apartment B."

"And is this vehicle your property?"

"Um . . . yes, sir."

"What is the make and model?"

He took her through some questions that seemed pointless, obvious and non-threatening, then asked her to account for her movements of the morning.

"Um . . . I got up— "

"What time, Miss?"

She went over her day from 7:45 until Alan Cunningham sent her to wait on the porch. No, nobody was with her during the night or in the early morning. Yes, somebody could verify she was at the coffee house. No, she hadn't stopped anywhere on the way there or on the way home. Yes, it was her habit to lock her car, but. . . .

Her mouth dried out and she got light-headed again but, just when she thought she'd have to sit down and ask for some water, the sheriff closed his notebook, asked her not to leave town, and said she could go in.

Her champions came with her. Kerry helped her up the stairs and took her keys from her trembling hands.

Chapter 11

Juss looked around Abby's apartment with the eye of a born sleuth — or a born none-of-your-businesser, as Granny Ruth used to put it. Self-help books on controlling anxiety *and* a complete set of Stephen King. Videos of relaxation techniques *and* what appeared to be every creepy movie ever made. Either this woman was a glutton for punishment, or one of her coping techniques was desensitization.

"Stay 'way from the window." Delaney's tenor voice almost sang it, drawing a chuckle from Juss. Abby reluctantly stepped back as he said, "Please sit down, Miss Andrews. Here on the couch, between Mr. Dashingly and myself."

"They're taking my car," Abby said, faintly.

"Yes, ma'am, they are." Delaney bent over a yellow pad, exposing the shiny bald patch he hid, whenever possible, under a hat. A fountain pen, almost invisible in his broad ebony fist, floated across the paper, leaving a glossy river of legal thought. "Fortunately, your cousin knows Miss Chocolate, and Miss Chocolate retains me. Therefore, they aren't taking *you*. That's the thing to remember."

"Yes. Thank you." Abby looked at each of them with watery eyes. "Um . . . do you want some tea or soda or something? Or coffee?"

"I'll make tea," Juss said, halfway to the kitchen before she had ended the sentence. "Everybody want tea? Abby, have you had lunch? DW, have you had lunch?"

Abby fidgeted, apparently torn between getting up to

play hostess and struggling against DW's request for her to sit down.

Juss patted her hostess on the shoulder. "No, Abby, you take it easy. I'll do it."

In the kitchen, she found more kinds of grocery store tea than seemed entirely healthy, most of it outdated. Juss made Earl Grey for herself, English Breakfast for DW and Kerry, and chamomile for Abby. No sugar bowl or cream pitcher — or cream, for that matter — so she scooped sugar into a coffee cup and poured powdered creamer into another. No tray, but there was a rusty cookie sheet. She spread a dish towel over that and loaded everything on, along with a plate of sandwiches made with store-bought pimiento cheese on spongey white store-bought bread.

She put the tray on Abby's chipped and stained coffee table, served everyone, and sat, snuggling deep into the armchair she'd commandeered. She beamed at the trio on the sofa as DW and Abby picked at the sandwiches and they all slugged down their tea. Two employees and a lady in distress. *Happy, happy.*

She'd met DW — Dexter Walter "Double Wide" Delaney back when Granny Ruth had had him break the clause in Great-grandmama's will forbidding "Harold and Bridget's wretched little love child" ever living in the Spadena Street house. That was when Juss and Doris had moved in with Granny Ruth to take care of her, and stayed to take care of the house when Granny Ruth had put herself into assisted living. They had kept in touch over this and that legality over the years, and now her having put him on retainer was proving to have been a good idea, because here he was, helping.

Delaney flipped to a previous page. "Miss Andrews, you have no idea what was taken from your car?"

She shook her head. "It looked like a rat. Black. Hairy. Long. Skinny. It was wearing a red collar."

He stared at her a moment, then looked back at his pad. "The questions the police asked you indicate that what they found might have something to do with Jack Pitt's death. Tell me again your connection to him."

Abby recited, as if repetition had made it as smooth as a water-worn stone, her tale of the accident, the state's automatic assignment of fault to her because she was uninsured, Pitt's determination to "make an example" of her, the multiple court dates, her termination from her job for time missed, the final hearing, and the criminal court judge's dismissal of the case.

"You never made any threats against Mr. Pitt? In person, over the phone, by email, or in writing? Explicit or implicit?"

"I called him a butt, but not to his face. To my lawyer and to my friends."

"Who was your lawyer?"

"Robert Byrum."

Delaney nodded. "Know him. He's small-time, likes it that way, good at it. May I ask why you didn't call him when the officer suggested you call someone?"

"I didn't think. I called Kerry, and. . . ."

"And he was with Miss Chocolate, and everything got away from you. I do understand."

"Blah," said Juss.

"Mr. Byrum didn't like Mr. Pitt, either," Abby said. "Neither did Judge Walkin."

Delaney looked up. "Byrum, Pitt and Walkin, Pitt

showboating on a driving uninsured case. This was in April? Judge Walkin had to excuse himself to make a phone call, cancel an appointment? This was that case?"

Although Delaney was usually as closed-mouth as a wooden oyster, Juss took a chance and asked, "Why?"

He surprised her by answering. "Judge and Mrs. Walkin had an appointment with an adoption agency that afternoon. The driving uninsured hearing should have been open-and-shut, but Pitt dragged it out and the Walkins had to reschedule. Word was, they were scared it would hurt their prospects."

"Oh, really?" Juss pulled a notebook and ballpoint from her purse. "Judge Walkin," she said, reading as she wrote. "Mrs. Walkin." She labeled the list and read: "Suspects."

Delaney scowled. "What do you mean, 'Suspects'?"

Juss ignored him and asked Abby, "Who else do you and Pitt have in common? Who else was in court that day?"

Abby made a helpless gesture. "Marsha Knowles."

Juss clicked her pen shut and open, shut and open. "Who's Marsha Knowles? S-h or c-i? MarSHa or MarCIa?"

"S-h."

"Mar-sha Knnnowwwles." She wrote it down. *Happy.* "And Marsha Knowles is?"

Kerry answered. "The other one. The one who hit Abby's car. She was like a witness for the state."

"Complainant," said Delaney.

Abby flushed pink at the memory. "When they said I was the one at fault because of the insurance, she claimed *I* hit *her*. I had witnesses, but Mr. Pitt took her lie into court. You should have seen them; it was disgusting. She sat there smirking, and he pranced around her making little jokes. Kerry and everybody thought that was why he made such a big deal, when he should have let me off with a fine and maybe driving school. He was trying to get me declared at fault so she could make me pay for her car, or so her insurance wouldn't raise her rates or something. Or just to make her happy. She seemed to get a kick out of it all, the bi— ." Abby's jaw squared up and firmed.

Why bless my soul, it's a woman, and not a jellyfish after all.

Delaney tapped his notes. "*That* was this case, as well?" Before Juss could ask, he said, "Word was, Pitt had a thing going with a complainant in a collision. Barbara Pitt moved in with her mother for a month — this was you, as well?"

Juss thought Abby seemed gratified that her case had been the talk of the bar lounge, or whatever they called the room where the lawyers hung out and drank coffee and swapped gossip. Although 'bar lounge' sounded like a place with dim lights and a jazz piano, so bar lounge was probably not what it was called. *Barbara Pitt.* She added the name to her list.

Aloud, she said, "So. Now all we need to do is prove who killed Jack Pitt."

"No," said Delaney, "now *I* need to keep Miss Andrews, here, from being charged or, if charged, from being convicted."

"But the best way to do that is to prove who did it."

"No, the best way to do that is to file her statement. An officer was on the spot the precise moment Miss Andrews opened her vehicle. Maybe he *happened* to be there, maybe not. Maybe he always carries a digital camera, maybe he doesn't. Search and seizure without a warrant is allowed if the property owner grants permission, but it's a *lit*-tle shady if the officer knows what he's looking for and the owner doesn't. 'The sneaky policeman tricked me' sometimes plays well with a jury."

"He wouldn't do that!" said Abby.

Oh, ho. "Do you know that cop?" she asked Abby.

Abby flushed again and shook her head, eyes on the floor.

Oh, ho, oh, ho! He is *kinda cute. If you like the type.*

Delaney grunted, mind working. "Miss Andrews, I'll meet you at the Justice Center at ten sharp tomorrow morning, so you can make your official statement. I'll have these notes typed and ready for you to sign, but they might have some questions of their own. They might want to go over everything themselves. If they do, tell it to them the way you told it to me today. Don't bring up anything about the trial. If they ask, give the facts. If they ask if you were angry with Pitt, you may say you weren't happy, but you know he was only doing his job. Don't get into the Marsha Knowles thing. We'll go over it a little more in the morning. For tonight, though, don't worry."

"I'll try." She managed a small, sickly smile.

Juss assured her, "Kerry and I will meet you there, too."

The lawyer frowned. "I see no need— "

"She needs moral support. You want your cousin there, don't you, Abby?"

Abby looked nervously at each of the others. "Well . . . yes." She twisted her fingers so hard, Juss was afraid she'd hear bones snap.

Kerry patted his cousin's hand. "I'll call Schatzi. I'm

sure you can stay with us for a while, until this thing is settled."

Abby relaxed ever so slightly, with a grateful look.

Apologetically, Kerry said, "Miss Chocolate, I'll call the agency right away and have another secretary sent out to you." He checked his watch. "Probably not until tomorrow, though."

"No!" Juss sat up so straight so suddenly she nearly slopped her tea. "I don't want another secretary!"

Kerry's face closed down. "But I'm afraid I simply can't make it," he said coldly. "I'm sorry, but family comes first."

"Well, *of course* it does! But you're still my secretary. Going to be with your cousin is in your job description."

The corner of his mouth twitched. "'And other duties as assigned'?"

"Exactly."

"Glad that's sorted out." When Delaney stood, the room felt barely big enough to hold him. "Juss, I'll walk you to your car."

"I'm not in my car. I came with Kerry."

"I'll call you a cab."

"I'm not ready to leave."

"Yes, you are." He stuck out his hand as Kerry and Abby rose. "Miss Andrews. Mr. Dashingly. Until tomorrow."

~*~

Out on the sidewalk, Juss regarded her attorney shrewdly. "I believe you know what it is, don't you? What they found."

He unlocked his car. "No, I do not."

"You suspect."

Delaney tugged at his hat brim and said, "Pitt thought it

made him look like a with-it young powerhouse to keep his hair shoulder-length and pull it back with a— " he flickered fingers toward his nape, " —hair thing. He favored red. I'm thinking that's Abby's 'rat with a red collar'."

"You don't think she did it, do you? I think no way."

"I think no way, too. I think it was planted."

"By the cop?"

Delaney was silent, looking thoughtful.

Juss, remembering the thin young man who had advised Abby to call for help, answered herself. "I think no way."

The lawyer smiled. "I think no way, too."

Juss smiled back, eyes glittering. "If Abby didn't put it there, and the cop didn't put it there, somebody else must have put it there. The killer."

Delaney's smile faded.

"That's for the police — Juss! That's for the police to discover. Don't give me that look. Juss, I have to deal with the police. Don't make it hard on me. Please."

"I won't."

DW looked unconvinced. He worked his shoulders, a sure sign he was about to make a concession. "We'll talk about it tomorrow after I get back from court."

We'll talk about it sooner than that. If you think I won't be there tomorrow morning with bells on, you don't know me very well.

"You'll be there tomorrow morning with bells on, won't you?"

"If it's okay with Abby."

"It'll be okay with Abby, by the time you get through with her." He sighed. "If it's all right with my client, you can come along for the ride, but you can't drive. Understand?"

"Of course."

She watched him pull away, smug in the reflection that he hadn't called a cab for her. She headed back to Abby's apartment.

Happy.

Chapter 12

Juss finished rinsing the casserole dish from supper and put it in the drainer. "Dishwashers are on sale this week. I saw it in the paper."

"We got four dishwashers," Doris said, holding up her hands. "I got two and you got two."

Juss cut them each a piece of buttermilk pie, topped up their mugs and sat down.

"Mmm!" Doris washed down a bite with a sip of coffee. "This is good, Baby Girl. You got a way with a crust."

"It didn't matter," Juss said, returning to their conversation. "Kerry had already called his wife, and Abby was packing and didn't want to talk. Maybe I can take them to lunch tomorrow after the Justice Center and get more information."

"What 'information'? Didn't you tell me DW told you to butt out?"

"I told Kerry not to worry about the work, that he needed to be there for his cousin."

"What 'work'?"

"I'll clock him in for a full eight hours every day. DW and I ought to clear this up pretty fast."

"DW *and you*?"

"Then, if it's agreeable with Kerry, I pay the buy-out fee to the temp agency, and Kerry can work for me."

"Doing what, may I ask?"

It wasn't like Doris to be so slow. "*Secretary*."

"You don't need a secretary. Once you clean the

upstairs, you got nothing in the world to occupy your time but garden and bake and tell people with more money than sense what to do."

Juss didn't answer. She couldn't, without being dishonest, because she was coming to doubt what she was doing. Not entirely — although a few of her clients were too lazy or stubborn or silly to figure out the obvious, most of them really needed help. Most of them were clueless or confused or didn't trust their own instincts and judgment. She was a *helper*. She *helped*.

Feebly, she said, "And he's going to catalog the library. Remember?"

"*That* could use doing."

"I'm going to my office. To *work*."

Granny Ruth had had a word for how Juss felt right now: heartsore. Why couldn't Doris understand? Why did she have to make light of what Juss did? It didn't help, that Juss shared parts of some of her goofier cases. But she couldn't share the serious ones. Those were important. And even if her clients should have had the sense to figure out their own answers, some of them were genuinely unhappy and she really, truly made their lives more liveable. She *did*.

~*~

The doorbell rang.

She straightened her suit jacket and fluffed her hair. *Might be a client. Might be Kerry. Might be a surprise.*

It was and it wasn't a surprise. It was one of the neighbors: the hose waver from the middle of the next block. Mrs. Tomahawk or something. Her first name had to do with her short, fuzzy white-blonde hair. *Dandelion?* Probably not Dandelion.

She looked like a businesslady paperdoll, in an off-white linen suit and a pink silk blouse with a pink and white enamel on gold lapel pin shaped like a dogwood branch. Her dusty rose lipstick was on slightly crooked. That, along with how rapidly she blinked her green hazel eyes and the way she fidgeted with her caramel-colored shoulder bag, caught Juss' interest and engaged her sympathy.

Maybe not a tourist. A friend of Doris' with a problem.

"Are you all eating? I can come back."

This lady looked a little worried. She looked a little sad.

Juss opened the door an inch wider and said, "No, we're done. Doris is in the kitchen. Come on back."

"I'm here to see you, actually," the lady said. She looked over her shoulder. "May I come in?"

A client! That's what a lot of them did — looked over their shoulders, like it was a shame to hire a Life Coach. According to Doris, it was.

"Certainly! Certainly! The office is this way. Please, come in and make yourself comfortable."

She settled the lady in the client's chair and snuggled into her Life Coach throne.

"What can I do for you?"

The new client pulled a gold card case from her bag, withdrew a business card, and stretched her pink fingers with their pink fingernails to hand it to Juss.

The card read M.A. Tomaneck, Real Estate.

Tomaneck, not Tomahawk, you goof!

"All right, Ms. Tomaneck, what seems to be the problem?"

50

"Well." She flicked a hand at her card. "I'm in real estate, and I do well enough. In fact, I do really well."

Juss smiled. "Is that a problem?"

Ms. Tomaneck held up her left hand and said, "Well, yes."

When Juss only looked at her, she lifted the hand higher and wiggled her fingers.

"I'm sorry," Juss said. "Could you—"

Ms. Tomaneck raised her right hand, stuck out her pointing finger and tapped it on her wedding band.

Juss hadn't a clue what that meant, unless it meant "call me MRS. Tomaneck," but she had a few of what she called (to herself) Life Coachy tricks. She tried one out now. She leaned back in her chair, steepled her fingers, smiled gently, and said,

"Mrs. Tomaneck, sometimes what seems to be a huge problem or difficult question becomes more manageable if you put it into words. I want you to do that for yourself."

She gestured toward Mrs. Tomaneck's hands, as if they both knew exactly what the charade word was.

Mrs. Tomaneck plopped her hands into her lap and heaved a big sigh. She opened and closed her mouth a few times, staring at the corner of the desk for inspiration. Then a smile crept across her face and she laughed.

"You're right," she said. Juss tried not to be offended at the astonishment in her voice. "Just thinking about saying it makes it seem so silly!" She shook her head. "See, Bee-Beep — Bobby — that's my husband — has always been the breadwinner, and I worked some when times were tight and because I like it, but he always brought home the bacon and I supplied the gravy. But now he's retired, and his pension and Social Security are real good, but now, like I said, he's not working, and I *am*. And I'm doing really well. I don't make what he's still bringing in from his pension and all, but I'm doing really well and I'm working."

"I see," said Juss, who didn't see the problem but could clearly see that Mrs. Tomaneck saw one.

"But you know what I could do?"

Juss hoped she wasn't going to say, *Quit working*. Doris would not be happy if she ever found out Juss had influenced anybody to work any less than they already did, unless they were working themselves to death.

"I could ask Bee-Beep — I mean Bobby — how he feels about it. He'd tell me the truth. He really would. And if he said he didn't mind and then he started minding, he'd tell me. He wouldn't tell me to quit, but he'd tell me if he minded. I could always cut back and make less if I had to."

Juss opened her mouth, but Mrs. Tomaneck went on.

"I'll make Bee-Beep's — Bobby's — favorite meal tomorrow night, meatloaf and mashed potatoes and corn cut off the cob and a green salad with those little white radishes and home-made Thousand Island dressing and a chocolate lava cake."

Please don't let my stomach rumble. I just finished eating, stomach!

Mrs. Tomaneck popped her hands together. "Then I'll ask him. If he says my income bothers him, I'll call my boss and tell him I'll be cutting back. If he says it doesn't, I'll keep chugging away like The Little Engine That Could and see if I can win that Best Sales Representative trip to Bermuda. Bee-Beep — Bobby — would like that. We could go swordfishing or whatever Bermudananians do."

Mrs. Tomaneck hefted her bag into her lap and opened it.

"Well, thank you *so much*. I wasn't sure this was such a good idea, but I was at my wits' end and Doris is always bragging about how smart you are."

She is?

"I'm so glad I decided to come! What do I owe you? Whatever it is, you've earned every single penny." She lifted an eyebrow at Juss. "If it isn't too much, of course."

Let's see, fifteen or twenty minutes and I said about ten words.

"I really didn't do anything, Mrs. Tomaneck. The answer was inside you all the time."

"But you knew how to get it out! And your time is worth something."

"I'll tell you what: Bring me a slice of that cake, and we'll call it even. I'll split it with Doris."

"Oh, that's a good idea!"

Juss walked her almost-a-client to the front door, personal details of the Tomanecks' life histories swirling around her like the aroma of fresh bread. Once Mrs. Tomaneck was on the stoop, she apologized for running off, wiggled her wedding band hand, and trotted down the walk and away.

Doris was still in the kitchen, making out a grocery list.

"Who was it at the door?"

"Guess!"

Not looking up, Doris said, "Santy Clause?" That was what she always guessed.

"It was one of the neighbors, actually, with a Life Coach problem!"

"Are you kidding me? One of *our* neighbors?" She looked up, and Juss could see her wanting to ask who and understanding Juss couldn't answer, if she asked. "I know, I know. Life Coach/Client privilege. All I can say is, if Chickapoo Tomaneck ever comes to see you, better have a shoehorn handy or you'll never get in more than ten words."

"Chickapoo!" Juss cackled and gave Doris a bear hug.

~*~

The doorbell rang again.

It was DW.

"May I come in, or are you mad at me for making you leave Abby's?"

She snickered and held the door wide. "As if I didn't know the way back in. The party was breaking up by the time I got upstairs again, anyway." Virtuously, she said, "I had to help clean up from lunch, didn't I?"

"You're all heart." He shucked off his coat and hung it on the coat rack and put his hat on top, like the star on a Christmas tree.

Juss served him pie and decaf while he and Doris exchanged greetings.

"So?" Juss asked. "Did you find out about the ponytail?"

"Never mind the ponytail. Let me handle this. This is law — serious law. It's outside your area of expertise. Agreed?"

"The law is outside my area of expertise, serious or not."

He nodded, satisfied, and they dropped into small talk about his wife and two grown sons.

After DW left, taking the rest of the pie with him, Doris stretched and said, "Going up to see what's on TV. Or might watch a movie. Coming? Or you got a date?"

Again, with the date!

"Who would I have a date with?"

Doris shrugged. "Thought you might have met somebody at the office furniture store or around your secretary's cousin's place."

"A girl gets hit on by strangers when she's young. Not so much, when she's middle-aged."

The dating. Oh, the dating. How many men had she been out with in her life — mostly before moving in with Granny Ruth? How many had she lived with? How many had drained her bank account, her heart, her energy?

Doris was different. Doris had good luck with men.

"What about you?" Juss asked. "Where's Herb tonight?"

"Wednesday. Herb's at church."

Doris, to her own and Juss' bemusement, had been keeping company for going on five years with an upright, church-going middle-class gentleman who worked in an honest-to-goodness hardware store on 17th Street. He wanted marriage, Doris didn't. Juss didn't give it much longer, and she felt bad for both parties.

Doris stroked Juss' cheek. "You can't let the bad ones put you off all of 'em. Maybe if you had a man, you wouldn't want to be poking in strangers' business so much."

Juss' inner teenager made her want to stomp away and slam a door, but her inner Life Coach, versed in clients' complaints, went *Ah-HA! Just like a mama to make you unhappy because she wants you to be happy!*

She gave Doris a mighty hug and patted her on the back with both hands. "Don't worry about me, Mama D. One of these days, Mr. Perfect will come along, and then you won't be able to sleep for the lovelight shining out of my eyes." She fluttered her lashes. "Besides, I like things fine the way they are."

~*~

In the office, Juss snuggled back into her padded executive chair and woke up her computer.

Before she touched the keyboard, though, she took a side road into the wilderness of *did* she like things fine the way they were? Did she wish she had married JohnnyO?

She shook her head, as if someone else had asked her out loud. JohnnyO was a nice guy. A great guy. He deserved a wife who loved him. Wanted him, like people are supposed to want their lovers.

She made a face and pushed at her keyboard as if it had tried to French kiss her.

Don't worry about it, Mama D used to say, when Juss had brought up how she felt — or didn't feel. *When you meet the right fella, you'll have the right feelings.*

But she never had. And women didn't light her fire, either. She got crushes on men, or had a little flutter over a man's gorgeous smile or wonderful eyes or pencil-thin mustache or cute backside. She was in the prime of life. Doris was right: She ought to be sowing wild oats like the free spirit she was, not sitting home watching television and working on the computer.

Which brought her back to Jack Pitt. She shuddered, thinking about the smarmy tomcat, grateful that she had never had to work with anybody like that, never had to put up with it for fear of losing a need-this-to-survive job.

She opened a new document, named it Jack Pitt Suspects, and saved it to a hidden folder. After a little thought, she built a table in the document with a column for *names* and columns for *motive, means, opportunity, alibi, connection to Abby* and *connection to Pitt*. With her notebook as reference, she filled in as many spaces as she could.

He was married with a daughter. Or stepdaughter? She switched to her browser and found one of the news stories about the murder, one with a little background. *Yeah. There it is.*

Barbara Pitt. Motive — jealousy? Connection to Pitt — wife.

Judge Michael Walkin. Motive — might have lost adoption? Connection to Abby — judge in driving uninsured case. Connection to Pitt — judge.

Mrs. Eleanor Walkin. Motive — might have lost adoption? Connection to Pitt — through judge.

Marsha Knowles. Motive — crime of passion? Connection to Abby — hit Abby's car, complainant in Pitt's DU case against Abby. Connection to Pitt — complainant in DU case against Abby, maybe lover?

She hesitated, then made a new row and inserted another entry.

Sharon Pitt. Motive — family matters? Connection to Pitt — daughter by deceased wife.

Means is always car. Maybe I should take that out. But Motive-Means-Opportunity was what they always had in detective shows and stories, so she decided to leave it in.

Now for the hard decision. *Should I put Abby in? No.* Abby was innocent. Juss didn't have to be impartial, and she wasn't going to be, and that was that.

Satisfied, she copied each name to the top of a page in her notebook.

Chapter 13

"Oh, sure," Schatzi said. "Everybody knows about Jack Pitt."

"I don't." Kerry finished buttoning his pajama top and slid into bed next to her.

Joel, Angie, and Lisa had been delighted with Abby's visit. Joel had caught a sense that she was upset, and had gone to bed troubled, but the younger two had been in a party mood, and hard to get settled down.

"You'd know about him, if you came to the Friends of the Library work parties. Donna knows all the dirt on everybody in town, just about. According to her, Jack Pitt might as well leave his pants at home."

"Good heavens!"

"I'll say. He was playing around with Barbara while he was still married to Laureen. Laureen put him through law school, worked full time *and* took care of the baby, and then, as soon as he started making money, it was *Goodbye, old chum, it's been good to know ya*. And then Barbara married him and was surprised — although nobody else in the world was — that he was playing around with somebody else. You'd think a woman would have the sense to know that if a man would play around *with* them, he'd play around *on* them."

"You'd think so."

Schatzi took a snore strip out of the drawer of her bedside table, dropped the wrappings next to the clock, and stuck the strip across her nose.

"She's back living with her mother," she said.

Kerry spoke through a yawn: "I thought she was dead."

"Who, Barbara or her mother?"

"I don't know. I lost track. The first wife."

"That was Laureen." Schatzi lowered her voice to a whisper. "She killed herself. Pills. On purpose, but they said it was an accident so Sharon could collect the insurance."

"Who's Sharon?"

"Laureen and Jack Pitt's daughter." She snapped her fingers three times. "Get with the program, Jasper!"

Kerry chuckled and yawned again.

"So," Schatzi said, "Barbara Pitt is living with her mother, Josephine Costa, who used to be Josephine Larimore. You know Max and Ashley Larimore. Well, Josephine is their father's younger sister, and she married a man from Milwaukee but he died of pneumonia last year."

"So Jack Pitt's current wife, Barbara, is in Milwaukee with her mother?"

"Now you got it. Yes."

"So I guess she didn't do it, unless she flew in from Milwaukee. Or hired a hit man."

"A hit man! Listen to you talk!" She shook a finger. "No more CSI for *you*, mister!"

She turned off her bedside light and yawned.

"G'night, sweetheart."

Kerry kissed her flannel-clad shoulder. "*Mwah!* Good night."

He turned out his own light, but lay awake, sorting out relationships and telling himself to trust Delaney. A high-priced lawyer like that — *High-priced. How is Abby going to afford a high-priced lawyer? We can help out, but can* we *afford it?* He resolved to muster his practicality tomorrow morning and ask Delaney what his fee would be. Schatzi would do it in a heartbeat. *Poor Abby.* He yawned and fell asleep.

Chapter 14

Injustice was at the Justice Center by 8:30. There were some other early birds milling around downstairs, faces strained or hopeful as they talked to each other or their attorneys. She waved to the people she knew and nodded to the people she didn't. None of them were her clients, she was glad to note.

She looked around for DW, but he wasn't there yet. An apparently casual scan of the building directory posted on a pillar told her where Judge Walkin's office was. She took the stairs to the third floor.

MICHAEL WALKIN was painted on the frosted glass of the door, with WALK IN underneath. Juss wondered how many jokes the judge and his clerk fielded over that.

A small sleek brunette looked up and smiled brightly. "May I help you?"

Juss leaned across the desk and said, softly, "Wanted to see how the adoption is going. Everything okay?"

The brunette's smile widened. "Oh, that came through months ago! She's the sweetest little thing! Mrs. Walkin had her in the other day, and she is precious."

One of the nice things about living in a small town was that nobody was surprised if you asked personal questions. They assumed you knew their mother's hairdresser or something and had a right to know.

"Terrible, about Jack Pitt," Juss said, "but when I think of him holding the judge up that time. . . ."

"Oh, my goodness, yes," the brunette said. "Mrs.

Walkin called and called to see what was keeping the judge. I thought she'd pop a gasket! You should have seen the judge fly out of here when he finished court. He was fit to be tied."

"But it didn't make any difference, I'm glad to see."

"No, it didn't, but the judge hasn't spoken to him outside of court since. Mrs. Walkin is so nervous, and that didn't help. Phoebe is a doll, though. The judge is in his chambers, or I'd sneak you in for a look at his pictures of her."

"Maybe another time. Thanks for the update."

"You're welcome."

Juss started out, but turned back and came to lean over the desk again.

"Speaking of Jack Pitt, did he ever hit on you?"

The brunette's eyebrows raised. "You too?"

"Don't act so surprised." Juss forced a chuckle to take some of the tartness out of her retort.

"Oh, I'm sorry, I'm sorry, that did sound bad, didn't it? I'm sorry. But he liked them. . . ."

"Young?"

The brunette blushed. "I was going to say petite. Short, I mean, like me. He married tall and flirted small, we always said."

"Who's 'we'?"

"The ones he hit on. We had kind of a club. The Pitt Hits." She giggled, then pressed her lips together. "I shouldn't laugh. Don't speak ill of the dead, my grandma used to say."

"Really? Mine, too."

"Really?"

"Mm-hmm."

The brunette put down her pen, so Juss made herself at home in a slightly padded metal chair. She could see a brass name plate now, with *Catherine Wheeler* etched into it. "Who all is in the club?"

"Oh, it wasn't anything formal, with dues or anything." Catherine flashed her bright smile. "Just something we'd joke about over coffee and that. We said he picked little gals, but he made up for it in volume. Lots of us, you know."

"He ever, you know, take it too far?"

Catherine's dark eyes flashed fire and her smile disappeared. "My grandma taught me not to speak ill of the dead. I'm not saying anything, so you can draw your own conclusions."

The phone rang and Catherine switched to professional mode.

Juss stood and they finger-waved to each other.

Back in the hall, Juss sat on a wooden bench and flipped open her notebook. On Mrs. Walkin's page, she wrote *Nervous* and *Phoebe*. On Judge Walkin's she wrote *Angry*, *Proud of Phoebe* and *Hasn't spoken to Pitt since Abby's trial*. Neither seemed to have much of a motive for murder, but you never knew. How nervous was nervous? How angry was angry?

She drew a heavy line under *Nervous* and one under *Angry*. They still didn't look like motives for murder.

On a blank page, she wrote *Pitt Hits* and *jealous of others*, *insulted* and *defending honor*. She drew a line across the page halfway down and headed that section *Pitt Hit Connection*, with the same motives listed. They didn't look very convincing, either, even written twice.

She wandered back down the stairs. On the second landing, she saw a familiar face — a young man in uniform.

The name popped into her head.

"Alan, isn't it? Alan Cunningham? You called it in about Abigail Andrews' car?"

He flushed and looked down. His bass voice rumbled, "Yes, ma'am."

He wishes it hadn't been him. Has our Abigail made a conquest?

"You were very kind to her," Juss said. "It was good of you to suggest she call for support."

He glanced up and down the stairs. "I can't talk about it. You know."

"Oh, sure, sure. Nice of you to put in a good word for her, too."

"Well, I made my report, you know. Told it like I saw it. You know, they train us to observe and report without, you know, no fear or favor and that."

"That's good. There must be a lot of pressure to nail the killer — extra, I mean, because of Pitt being a DA."

"Well, yes and no." The young man hitched up his belt.

Must be hard to keep all that equipment up when you don't have any hips.

He went on solemnly, in a tone that told Juss he did a lot of elementary school Career Day talks.

"We take every crime seriously. You look at a cop, and you see all this equipment like on this belt and you think it's all glitter and glamor, but we see some sad things out there, and it's all important to us. A crime on a poor person or a old person or a young person like yourself — " Juss appreciated that — "is just as important as a crime on the richest taxpayer in the world or the most important person. We don't rush to judgment when a crime is committed, but hold off and actually think about it and gather clues and things like that."

Should I ask? Worth a try. "So what did you find in Abby's car?"

He opened his mouth, but his brain engaged before anything came out. "I can't tell you that, ma'am. Sometimes, you know, we hold things back from the public in case some nut job makes a false confession. It wasn't anything dangerous or potentially harmful to the public good, you know. We wouldn't do that."

"Glad to hear it."

"Yes, ma'am. But, like I told them at the scene and like I put in my report, Miss Andrews didn't seem to me, in my trained official opinion, you know, she didn't seem to me to have any idea what that thing was. I was cycling by on patrol when she opened that door, you know, and she whooped like she'd been goosed and jumped back. She had no idea, and I'd swear to that in court."

"I'll tell her."

He blushed. "You know her?"

"I do."

He checked his watch. "I'm real sorry, I'm not being rude, you know, but I got some business to take care of here before I go out on patrol."

"Oh, sure, I didn't mean to keep you. Thanks again."

"I'd swear to it in court."

"I'll tell her."

They waved and he trotted up the steps.

Chapter 15

Kerry was glad to get to the Justice Center.

Abby had been sitting at the kitchen table, looking like she hadn't slept, when he and Schatzi had gotten up. She had made a pot of her signature watery coffee and had turned half a dozen slices of perfectly good ham into roof shingles.

She had gone over the court case and the discovery of whatever-it-was in a repeating loop, with enough variation that he couldn't even fall into familiarity with it and tune it out.

Schatzi had whispered, "There's a new star in your crown in Heaven," as she hugged him goodbye.

The drive into town had not been any better.

So Abby's panic at having to be scanned at the Center's entrance the same as everybody else provided a little relief.

He looked around for Juss, certain she would be there before them, and saw her coming down the stairs.

"There's Juss," he said, to distract Abby, and was surprised at his twinge of jealousy when Abby cried, "Oh, thank God!" and held out her arms to her new champion.

Juss gathered Kerry's cousin into a comforting embrace and winked at him over Abby's shoulder. Kerry couldn't have explained how that wink managed to communicate *We'll take care of this poor dear wounded rabbit together as a team*, but it clearly did.

"Not a word, not a word," a tenor voice called, and Kerry felt a strong hand land on his shoulder and give it a gentle squeeze.

DW Delaney took off his hat and stuffed it into his pocket, his eyes on Juss.

"Abby, I need to talk to you." He held out a hand, giving Juss no choice but to release her captive so Abby could turn and extend her own. "Have you been here long?"

"Um . . . we just got here," Abby said.

"I ran into that young policeman," Juss said. "The one who called in the report and told Abby to call somebody?"

"Alan Cunningham?" Abby looked around.

Oh, really? Kerry raised an eyebrow at Juss, who wiggled both of hers.

"He wanted me to tell you he believes you didn't know what was in your car, that you were shocked and surprised, and that he would swear to it under oath."

"You talked to him," Delaney said. "You questioned him."

"I ran into him by chance," Juss said virtuously. "We talked. People talk, you know. He volunteered the information."

Kerry didn't know his new employer well enough to be certain, but he had a strong suspicion that Juss had orchestrated the volunteerism, if she hadn't asked directly.

"That's good, isn't it?" Abby appealed to Delaney. "Isn't that good?"

"That's very good," Delaney said. "So long as the prosecution—" he held out a calming palm, "—if any — doesn't establish that his testimony was solicited." He glared at Juss, who said, "It wasn't," a bit weakly.

Kerry cleared his throat. His face felt hot, but he knew from Schatzi's assurance that he never blushed, no matter how embarrassed he felt.

"I'm afraid. . . ," he said, "uh . . . I must ask. . . . I'm sorry if it's in poor taste, but I'm afraid . . . uh. . . . Mr. Delaney, I'm not certain we can afford your fee. Your quite justifiable fee, I'm sure. We would if we could, of course, but, well, it's best to discuss these things, er, up front, don't you think?"

Juss said, "Don't—" but Delaney waved her to silence.

"Mr. Dashingly, my fee has been arranged between myself and Miss Chocolate. I am satisfied that I shall be satisfactorily compensated. Now I'm going to take Miss Andrews into that alcove over there and go over her statement with her. If you and Miss Chocolate want to discuss your repaying her, be my guest." With a smug little bow, Delaney took Abby's elbow and led her away.

"Really," Kerry said, "I don't think we can afford—"

Juss growled. Literally. "Grrrrrrr!" Her savage scowl was disarmed by the moistness in her eyes. She frowned at the floor.

"Miss Chocolate—"

"Juss!"

"Juss, then." It distressed him to have been part of her discomfort, but he knew Schatzi wouldn't flinch from the discussion. "We have some money saved, and naturally it's at our family's disposal, but—"

"I have a lot of money," Juss said, as if she were saying, *I have a headful of lice*, still giving the floor a dirty look.

"I'm very happy for you, but Schatzi and I *don't* have a lot of money. Nor does Abby." He wished she would

68

look at him. "I think we'd better retain an attorney we can afford."

"DW's free," Juss said.

"Oh, now—"

"He is! Well, not free, but I pay him a retainer. Keep him on retainer, you know? I pay him, whether he does anything or not. So he doesn't charge me anything when he *does* do something. See?"

"I don't think that's how it works."

"That's how it works with us," Juss said firmly. "So never mind." She ran a hand through her rumpled hair. "I understand," she said. "I do. Believe me, I'm not trying to play Lady Bountiful here. I *hate* that! Look, you know how you didn't even think, when Abby called? She didn't have to ask if you'd help her. She knew and you knew. You're family, and you're going to help. Right?"

"Right."

"Well, the way I was raised, you don't get born into a family, you *choose* your family. My parents. . . . It's complicated."

Kerry wished he hadn't said anything. He would have bitten a piece out of his tongue to take back his objection and spare her this.

"Doris told me something about it," he said.

She nodded, looking somewhat relieved. "Well, I choose you. And Abby."

Before he could stop himself, he said, "Why? I reported for work at random yesterday."

"I just do. Is that okay?" Juss tugged at the strap of her purse and seemed to search for words. "You've eaten at my table."

Kerry nodded. He understood that. He hadn't done

it deliberately, but he had obviously — fortuitously — stumbled onto the exact person to come to Abby's rescue where his own ability ended. Schatzi would call it Providence. That was as good a label as any.

"I really do have DW on retainer," Juss said, "and I really would be paying him, whether he did this or not. He wants to do this. And I want to do this. Okay?"

Schatzi always said it was mean to turn down an open-hearted gift.

"Okay," he said, telling his pride to sit down and shut up. "And thank you."

Juss' happy emu look was back.

"So listen to what I found out when I talked to Judge Walkin's clerk."

"Sh-sh!" Kerry saw Delaney coming back, Abby floating in his wake.

And suddenly, he was a co-conspirator. After all, what was he to do? Tattle? *Mr. Delayyyy-ney, Juss talked to Judge Walkin's cler-erk. I don't think she was supposed to do that, was she? Is she in trouble?* No, that was beneath consideration. So he tucked away a smile when Juss mouthed *Later*.

"I think we've got everything sorted out," Delaney said. "We'll go upstairs and take care of this. Miss Chocolate, you don't really need to be here."

"I don't mind. Can I come?"

"No."

"I've never seen anybody give a statement. I'd like to see that."

"No, Juss. You stay here."

"Oh, DW! Okay, then. I'll stay here."

Juss watched Abby and the lawyer walk away, then

grasped the sleeve of Kerry's suit jacket and pulled him to a bench.

"It's too bad he wouldn't let you—" he began, but she snorted as she pulled a notebook out of her purse and flipped it open in a gesture that put him strongly in mind of the sheriff.

"I didn't want to go, I wanted to make DW say *you stay here* instead of *you run along*. Listen to what I found out."

She read from the notebook, filling in details and flying off onto tangents. He told her what Shatzi had said about Pitt and his wives, current and ex.

"Okay," Juss said, contemplating her notebook. Kerry thought she looked daunted as she said, "That's a lot of suspects. And we don't even have names for the Pitt Hits or their significant others."

Kerry cleared his throat. "If I might make a suggestion. . . ."

"Sure."

"We're looking in one direction. Maybe this didn't have anything to do with his amorous peccadilloes."

"His what?"

"Playing around."

"Ah."

"He wasn't the only prosecutor. I mean, I know he isn't *the* Prosecutor, because that's Ed Prothero. I don't remember ever seeing Jack Pitt for Prosecutor on a yard sign in any election season."

"You're right. Where's the prosecutor's office? The directory is over here."

Kerry followed Juss to the directory. It was arranged in alphabetical order by office name, and he tapped the

Prosecutor cluster. Under the Prosecutor, there was a sub-entry of Chief Deputy Prosecutor and, under that, an entry for Assistant Deputy Prosecutors.

Juss pointed to the s at the end of Assistant Deputy Prosecutors.

"Plural," she said. "I wonder how many?"

"Let's find out." Kerry pushed the elevator call button, pleased at the approval on his employer's face. *This is fun.* He hadn't done field research since college. It was how he had met Schatzi, in fact. His assignment had been to interview fifty random people in town about their reading habits, then, assuming (as part of the exercise) they were all patrons of the same library, stock that imaginary library with 10,000 books to serve their needs using Bowker's Books in Print as a resource. Schatzi — Gretchen Alice Metzenberger — had been one of the random people he had interviewed.

On the fourth floor, he waved a hand for Juss to exit first and followed her down the hall to the door with PROSECUTOR carved into the lintel above it. Another directory was bolted to the wall beside the door, with titles and names on slide-in plates behind a locked Plexiglas cover. Juss took her notebook out and copied the information.

Kerry read: Prosecutor — Ed Prothero; Chief Deputy Prosecutor — Caroline Lewis; Assistant Deputy Prosecutors — David Blaine, Margery Wellington, Jack Pitt, Brenda Sue Gettlebarger.

"Shall we go in?" he asked, and was rewarded by a bright smile. Then the smile faded.

"I can't. No telling when DW and Abby will come back, and he'll know I didn't go home. There's only so far you can push people. I don't want to do something on purpose I know is going to make him mad."

"What would he do if he got mad?"

Juss cocked her head and gave him that *hel-looo* look Schatzi used on him sometimes. "He'd get mad." She took his arm as if they were a lady and a gentleman and led him back to the elevator. "I forget," she said. "You don't know how far back DW and Doris and I go. I pay his firm money and he does legal work for me, but DW and I are friends. He's a little bit bossy and I'm a little bit defiant because we met when I was young and he was already a grown-up, but we're friends."

Kerry wondered if Juss had any friends her own age. There was something sad and immature and lonely about her, rather like Abby without the high anxiety.

Back on the ground floor, with no Mr. Delaney or Abby in sight, Kerry consulted the directory again.

"*Hm*mmmm," he said.

"What? What?"

"The Personnel office is down here."

"Kerry, we can't investigate everybody who works in this building."

"No, but we can find out at least how many people work in the Prosecutor's office. The directory upstairs only listed the Prosecutors themselves. They're bound to have law clerks and secretaries."

"But DW—"

"You wait here. If he comes back while I'm gone, tell him the truth — I'm trying to drum up business for Louisa Bradley Temporaries and specifically for myself once the job with you runs out." She hesitated, and he said, "I know you'd rather do it yourself, but it has to be me."

"That's not—" She gave him the notebook and pen.

The Personnel office was at the end of a side corridor. The door was open, so he walked in and rested the notebook on the counter, drawing a business card from his inside suit coat pocket as a smiling middle-aged woman approached.

"How are you this morning?" he said.

"Can't complain. How about you?"

"I'm very well this morning. Beautiful day."

She glanced out of the window behind her and turned back to him with a genuine smile. "It sure is. What can we do for you this morning?"

He handed her the card.

"I'm a temporary office worker for Louisa Bradley Temporaries. I currently have an assignment, but if I find myself near or in a place that looks interesting, I often check to see if they ever employ temporaries. I've always been rather interested in the law, but I confess I lack the courage to contemplate police work. I'm not even certain I could be a dispatcher, taking calls from people in desperate trouble and getting the right unit there in time."

The woman chuckled. "I don't think things get all that hairy around here, but I see what you mean."

"What about the Prosecutor's office? Do they ever employ temporaries for secretarial work?"

"They try not to, because of privacy, you know."

"Certainly. All Louisa Bradley Temporaries are bonded, and I've worked for them for five years, in financial institutions and hospitals and other offices that require discretion. They do employ secretaries in the Prosecutor's office?"

"Oh, yes. Marydee has been with them since the Year Dot, and Ashley has been there, oh, ten years, at least."

"Only two secretaries for all those Prosecutors?"

"One Prosecutor, one Chief Deputy Prosecutor, four Assistant Deputy Prosecutors, three law clerks, two paralegals and two secretaries. The paralegals usually fill in if one of the secretaries is off."

Her phone rang. She flourished his card. "I'll keep this, though, in case something comes up."

As she picked up the phone, Kerry scribbled, *Marydee, yr dot* and *Ashley, 10+* and *3 law, 2 para.*

He only had time to hand the notebook back to Juss before Mr. Delaney and Abby came back. Abby looked much better than he had expected, and he gave DW credit for that. Not many people could have taken Abby through a distressing new experience and brought her out relatively calm.

"Mr. Dashingly, I turn your cousin over to you. She did very well for herself." He patted Abby gently on the shoulder. "Juss, I'll walk you to your car. I'm assuming Mr. Dashingly will take his cousin back to his place or wherever she wants to go."

"Sure," Juss said. "But hold on a minute. I was about to give Kerry a list."

"A list of what?"

"Stuff I want him to bring me when he comes to work."

This was news to Kerry, but he wasn't able to look over Juss' shoulder to see what this list was because Mr. Delaney herded the cousins into a group that excluded her.

"Mr. Dashingly, I've already advised your cousin to not leave town. She isn't accused of anything or even, so far as I know, suspected of anything, but we do know that something is going on, and being accessible to the police

— with adequate legal representation, of course — will be to her advantage."

Kerry nodded, as did Abby, her eyes as wide as those of that cartoon cat she liked so much.

"If the police should contact either of you, it might be better to decline to speak without your lawyer present." He put a large hand on his own chest, then reached into his inner suit coat pocket and pulled out a polished red card case. He gave each of them a card.

Dexter Delaney, Attorney at Law. There was something very reassuring about the words, though Kerry judged that the reassurance probably came from the words' association with Delaney himself.

Kerry gave Mr. Delaney one of his own cards, printing his home and cell phone numbers on the back in neat black letters.

"Abby will probably either be with me or with Schatzi. If she and Schatzi are out somewhere, we have an answering service."

"Machine," Abby said.

"Yes — machine."

"He always says 'service'."

There was the sound of paper ripping and Juss tucked a folded sheet from her notebook into Kerry's handkerchief pocket. He rearranged the careful folds of his handkerchief.

Mr. Delaney shook hands with Kerry and Abby. "I hope we'll meet again under more pleasant circumstances," the lawyer said, "and not at all in conjunction with whatever this is. Ready to go, Juss?"

"Sure." She sketched a wave at the cousins. "See you."

Kerry, holding his handkerchief in place, withdrew Juss' paper and unfolded it. The list read:

Bring

Abby

to

my

house?

Chapter 16

"What is *up* with this woman?" Schatzi's raised voice tickled his ear and he hoped Abby didn't hear her. He and his cousin were sitting in his parked car — he never spoke on the phone while he was walking or driving. "Is she, like, *How To Buy Friends and Influence People* or what?"

"No, she's generous and kind and she's taken an interest. Her ... friend, mother figure, housekeeper, whatever — Doris — says she's a people junkie. I suppose Abby is her current drug of choice." He winked at Abby, who was staring at him as if she thought she could hear Schatzi's half of the conversation if she only looked hard enough.

"Abby is?"

"Yes."

"Abby?"

"Yes," he said, firmly.

"Okay, I trust your judgment," Schatzi said, sounding as if she had strong doubts.

The phone beeped.

"You have another call?" Schatzi asked. "Better take it — might be about the kids."

It was Juss.

"I'm phoning my wife," he told her.

"Can she come, too? Ask her to come, too."

He switched lines. "I told her I was talking to my wife, and she instantly asked me to invite you along."

"Hmmph."

"It's that caaaastlllle." He dangled the prospect like a catnip toy in front of a kitten.

"All right. I'll meet you there, and bring Abby home if you ever do any work for this woman. See you soon, Sweetheart."

The cell phone didn't click on disconnection, but he could tell she was gone by an emptiness where she had been.

"Juss? Are you there?"

"Sure."

"Schatzi said she'd be delighted. The kids are in school, so—"

"You have kids?"

"Yes, three." *And, no, you may not send them to private school, summer camp, prep school, college, and Europe.* "I need to go now. Schatzi might feel uncomfortable, if she gets there before I do." *Not likely.*

Chapter 17

Juss wanted to update her suspects list. She went into the office, but left the door open so she would know when Kerry came.

The visit to the courthouse had turned up untold numbers of possible suspects, including a round dozen in the Prosecutor's office alone. And what if it wasn't any of them? What if it was his Sunday School teacher or his daughter's roommate or his butcher or somebody she had no way of knowing about?

But no, it can't be — not unless this is a coincidence too wild to be fair.

That made her wonder about all the suspects on the list. There were only two of them who were connected with Abby — so far as she knew: Judge Walkin and Marsha Knowles, the ... What was it? ... complainant in the driving uninsured case. But Abby was coming over, and so was Kerry's wife, who might possibly know something about some of these other people.

The doorbell rang. She hit "print" and hopped up to answer.

It was Kerry and Abby.

"Hi, come in, come in! Doris is out — this is her day to volunteer at the clothes closet. I used to, but they said I was too intrusive. Said I made the clients nervous."

"I can't imagine," Kerry said.

"Come into the office. Take a seat. I'll make some chicken salad for lunch when Mrs. Dashingly gets here, if that's okay." *Mrs. Dashingly. Sounds like a Jane Austin heroine.* "Abby, take a look at this and see if there's anybody on it you know. Other than Judge Walkin and Marsha Knowles, I mean."

While Abby looked the chart over, Juss got coffee for them all, putting Kerry's and Abby's on small check-writing tables built onto the arms of their chairs. She lowered herself into her late grandfather's Executive Deluxe Swivel and Rock. She snuggled back and beamed. *Happy!*

"Um. . . . I know Sharon Pitt a little. She used to go to the same church I did until she moved."

"Did you know each other to see, or were you friends?"

"Um. . . . We were friendly, but we weren't friends. We talked sometimes — you know, at church meals, or we'd talk in a group."

"Did she know your car? The one the police took, I mean?"

"I don't know. Why?"

"I'm just asking. Did you know her mother?"

"No, she had passed before I met Sharon."

"Did Sharon ever say anything about her? Or about her father?"

"No, but I heard somewhere that she and her father didn't get along."

Now we're getting somewhere. "Didn't get along how?"

"Um. . . ." Abby thought, brow furrowed. "I don't know. I can't remember any details. I just have an impression that he was hard to get along with. Or maybe I'm remembering it that way because he was such a butt to me."

"Hearsay," said Kerry.

"That's inadmissible in court," Juss said. "Not in gossip." She swiveled back toward Abby. "Can you remember who told you about them not getting along?"

Abby shook her head, her hair flying wild.

The doorbell rang again.

"Bet that's your wife." Juss jumped up. "Will she want coffee? Will you get it for her?"

The woman at the door was shorter than Juss by a few inches. Her shoulder-length bobbed hair was a deep rich red and her eyes were a deep rich blue.

Ooo, pretty!

"Hi, I'm Juss," Juss said, offering her hand.

The woman smiled and took the hand. "Greta Dashingly. I'm Kerry's wife."

Juss stood back. "Come in. We're in the office." She waved an arm toward the office door, inviting Scha — Greta to precede her. "Kerry talks about you all the time. I'm so glad to meet you!"

"And I'm glad to meet you, Miss Chocolate."

"Call me Juss, please."

Kerry had placed a chair for his wife— No, after a brief joining of hands and an exchange of eye contact that looked like an invisible embrace, he directed her to the chair he had been in and he sat in the chair he had added. Now there was an arc, so the three of them could see each other.

"Juss, can I get you anything while I'm up?"

"No, I'm fine." She went around and slumped in her one chair on the other side of the desk from the family trio. "So."

"Schatzi," Kerry said, "we were wondering about these people." He tapped the paper in Abby's hand. "Juss," he said, "why don't you bring your notebook around so you can show her what these notes mean to you?" He pulled another chair in from the waiting room and put it on the other side of his, waving her to the one he'd placed for himself.

When all the chairs and cups had been rearranged yet again, Juss was nestled inside the family row. *Happy!*

Abby gave Scha — Greta the printout of the suspect list and Juss turned to a new page of her notebook.

Greta ran a finger down the list. "Annnd why are we doing this?"

The strained look that had gone from Abby's face snuck back.

"Because," she said, "Jack Pitt was killed, and the police found something in the back of my car that makes me a suspect."

"They couldn't possibly—"

"They do! I know they do! They asked me what I did all morning, what time I got up and who saw me and all that. Mr. Delaney will do everything he can, but they . . . might . . . arrest . . . me."

Her voice had gotten breathier until she had to stop and gulp air.

"That's nonsense," Greta said. She tucked a wisp of hair behind Abby's ear.

"The police took my car," Abby whispered.

"And they'll look at it with their magnifying glasses, and it will tell them you didn't hit anybody with it." Greta turned back to the list. "I know Jean Louise Young and Carlton Cornflower. Jean Louise is a Friend of the Library — an active one — and Carlton is a counselor at that day camp Joel went to last summer and the year before. Kerry, you've met him — remember?"

"Oh, yes," Kerry said. "I thought I merely recognized him from the paper. He seemed nice."

"Before we signed Joel up, I asked around about the staff. The consensus was that Carlton was never the brightest color in the rainbow, but he's far from stupid. Very responsible and capable."

"Does he work by the book?" Juss asked.

Greta hesitated, then said, "I would say yes, for the most part. He was known for following the rules."

"And that's why we're doing this," Juss said. "In case the rules say he has to treat Abby like a suspect, whether he really suspects her or not. *If* DW can't build his own legal fence around Abby, we'll have something to give him that might help."

The easing of Abby's breath and the touch of color that came back to her face was better than a Pulitzer Prize. Greta's nod and her return to the suspect list put a Nobel on top of it.

"Barbara," she said, "I don't know. Sharon, I don't know."

"She went to my church," Abby said.

"So she did. I might have met her once, but I don't know her."

"Me neither."

"Judge Walkin and Eleanor, I've met. They brought the baby . . . What's her name? . . . Phoebe to the last Unity in Diversity meeting about interracial adoption. Phoebe's bi-racial or tri-racial or something. Cute as a button."

Juss turned back to her notes. "His clerk, Catherine Wheeler, said Pitt almost made the judge late for an adoption appointment and he and Mrs. Walkin were very upset."

"You have Cathy on the suspect list?"

"You know her?"

"Oh, yeah, Cathy and I go way back."

"Well, I thought, you know, loyal employee, and all that. Sometimes other people get more upset for us than we get for ourselves. Then, too, she was one of the women Pitt sexually harassed."

"Oh, Lord, yes. They say that that man had more hands than an octopus."

"Actually," Kerry said.

"Don't say it," Greta interrupted. "I know octopusses don't have hands. AND I know the plural is octopodes."

Kerry chuckled and Greta went on perusing the list.

"Let's see. . . . 'Pitt Hits'?"

"That's a club Cathy Wheeler told me about, of women Pitt hit on a lot."

"It's a stretch," Greta said. "Most women today don't take that kind of abuse. Maybe if there's one or two women up against a boss, with nobody to witness or back them up. Or if everybody around enables the abuser. But the courthouse women knew what he was like and watched out for each other around him. Even other men took him aside and told him to knock it off. He'd laugh and claim he wasn't doing anything. Cathy said he'd rub your shoulder, or run a hand down your arm or rub your back, but he was more about looks and smarmy remarks. He'd probably zero in if he thought he could get away with it, but I didn't get the impression from Cathy that he needed to be put down. And she *likes* the Walkins, but she wouldn't kill for them."

"What about the Walkins? Did Cathy ever talk about the thing with Pitt in court?"

"They said the whole process was difficult, but that it was good for the kids if the agency was careful, and that the difficulty was all in the past and forgotten. I said it sounded like childbirth, and Mrs. Walkin cried a little and said people didn't understand, that adopting a baby wasn't like buying a refrigerator, it *was* more like giving birth. It was very moving."

"Okay." In the margin of her notebook, next to her notes from her talk with Cathy Wheeler, Juss wrote, *Greta says no to Walkins and Wheeler and Pitt Hits.* "What about boyfriends or husbands of the Pitt Hits? Do you think it would do us any good to get a list and see if anybody's hot-headed enough to do an impulse hit-and-run?"

"Hmmmm. That's a maybe. That's a *maybe*. Who else have we got? Oh, Marsha Knowles. That stinker."

"You know her? I mean, besides from the trial?"

"No, I'm happy to say. She's one of those Highgate Commons exclusivites who work in the big city and wouldn't even drive through town if there were a way around it. They don't read the local paper or listen to the local news or shop the local stores. You never even see them in the grocery, because they shop at the big Kroger in Jefferson Point between here and the river. You know Highgate Commons?"

Oh, yes. "My great-grandmother lived there."

Greta winced. "Open mouth, insert foot."

"It's okay. That's exactly what she was like."

"So you know Marsha Knowles?"

"No, no. I never spent much time out there." *Like half an hour.* "Great-grandmama and I had differences." She could feel herself getting hot, thinking of those intense thirty minutes.

To her surprise, Kerry grinned.

"Doris told me what you called her." He repeated it to

Greta: "A 'running-dog flunky'."

"A running-dog flunky of the Capitalist/Industrialist system," Juss corrected him. "Did she also tell you what Great-grandmama called her? Called Doris?"

"No."

"She called her my 'Mammy'." Her hands curled into fists, and her head felt swollen with the rage that had inflamed her then and inflamed her again, every time she replayed the scene in her mind. She forced her hands to relax. "Lucky for Great-grandmama I was raised as a pacifist. Yeah, words can kill." She felt like she had derailed the spirit of the meeting, so she pushed the memory aside and said, "I was only there the once while Great-grandmama was alive. Then I went a couple of times with Granny Ruth after she inherited. She rented it out, and I went with her to meet the renters. Then Doris and I went out after Granny Ruth passed away to tell the people who were renting that they could stay. They seemed nice enough. A lot nicer than Great-grandmama, although that's damning with faint praise."

Greta, who impressed Juss as striding on stilts above the emotional cesspit of Great-grandmama's legacy, said, "So you might know someone who knows Marsha Knowles. You have an 'in' at Highgate Commons, anyway."

And the mood was back on track.

"Yes! I never would have thought of that."

"Yes, you would," said Kerry.

"Well, maybe eventually." She turned to a fresh page and wrote *Highgate Commons — Marsha Knowles lives there — who knows her?*

"Wait a minute," Greta said. "Why is Marsha Knowles on this list in the first place? Pitt was on her side."

"Maybe he went farther than a pat on the back with her. Maybe she didn't like it. Maybe she didn't like it a lot."

Abby shook her head. "She was simpering at him in court, lapping it up when he joked around with her and, you know, licked his lips at her and all that."

Juss didn't want to give up another suspect. "The main reason is the thing the police found in the back of Abby's car. If it does have to do with Pitt's murder, somebody planted it. Marsha is the only person so far who knew Pitt *and* Abby *and* might want to pin the crime on her."

"Makes sense. Who else is on here? The entire staff of the Prosecutor's office?"

Kerry said, "Workplace tensions? Completely unrelated to Abby's case, except that any of them would be aware of his cases and could pick someone to frame."

"Oh, you clever boy! Let's see. Ed Prothero likes his full eight hours. I've heard people who know him say the reason he doesn't hunt is that he won't get up before seven. When was Jack Pitt killed?"

"They haven't released that yet. Early yesterday morning."

"Mmmm. Okay. Chief Deputy Prosecutor Caroline Lewis. I've said hello to her, chit-chatted with her at various meetings, but I don't know her and don't know anything about her. David Blaine, Assistant Deputy Prosecutor, I know fairly well. He's the one you want to have *against* you in court. He's a 'benefit of the doubt' guy. Margery Wellington and Brenda Sue Gettlebarger. Margery is on the library's Board of Directors, but I don't know her. Vicky would, though. She's the Friends of the Library's Board Liaison. Brenda Sue shops at Fedora's a lot. I know her from there."

"Fedora's?" It was Juss' favorite shop, full of new and gently used jewelry, clothes, accessories, and art. "I love that place! I never saw you there."

"I work the evening shift Wednesday, Friday, and Saturday, after Kerry gets home to look after the kids."

"That is so cool! I would love to work there!"

"I'll have Kerry bring you an application."

Juss smiled back at Greta, wondering if the smile looked as forced as it was. *How could somebody with my means justify taking a job away from somebody who needs to make ends meet?*

"Or drop in between six and nine in the evening," Greta said. "I'll show you some bargains most people overlook."

"That, I'll do. I couldn't work there — I have my work. But I'd appreciate it if I could leave some cards on your counter."

"I'll ask. I sure will. Life Coach, isn't it?"

Juss got the feeling that Greta and Doris were separated at birth. A little defensively, she acknowledged the title.

Kerry had made tick marks beside the names as Greta went through them. "We didn't get the names of the clerks and the paralegals," he said. "I got the secretaries' names."

Greta said, "Oh, yes, Ashley and Marydee. I'm in book club with them. You'd think after working together all day, they'd want to get away from each other, but those two are joined at the hip."

"So," Kerry said, "you could talk to them about Pitt and about the other people in the Prosecutor's office."

"I could do that, yes."

"Will you?"

Greta glanced at Abby's hopeful face and said, "Of course."

Juss marked her copy of the list. "When does your club meet again?"

"Tuesday."

"So you'll talk to Caroline Lewis if she comes into Fedora's?"

"Yes."

"And Ashley and Marydee at book club?"

"Yes."

"And I'll go out to Highgate Commons and see what I can pick up about Marsha Knowles."

"And what will *I* do?" Kerry asked.

There was a moment of silence.

"Catalog my library?" Juss said.

"I meant what will I do for Abby, but, yes, I fully intend to do my job."

I sounded like a boss. I sounded like Great-grandmama.

Greta clucked her tongue. "So frosty. Such a frosty man."

Juss was relieved to hear Kerry clear his throat and say, "That did come out sounding rather stuffy, didn't it? I apologize. I'll clock in and get to work right after lunch, if that's amenable with you."

"Is 'amenable' like 'copacetic'?"

"Yes, except that it's a real word."

Greta elbow-nudged her just enough to invite her to appreciate the Kerryness of the remark.

Juss checked her watch. "I'm hungry. Anybody else?"

Everybody was.

~*~

90

Gathered around the table and after they had joined hands for Juss' one-size-fits-all cosmic thank you, they got back to work.

"What else?" Juss asked. She shook her head and tapped the suspect list next to her plate. "Oh, yeah: Whoever did this knows Abby and wants to pin this on her. We talked about that a little. But we didn't talk about when whoever-it-was planted whatever-it-was in your back seat."

"It could have been any time. Any time after the m-murder, anyway. I *think* I always locked my car, but I m-might have forgotten."

Juss wished she could comfort Abby's uncertainty, but she could tell it was a gaping chasm that could only be filled from the bottom up, from the inside out.

So, she passed over it and said, "That's not a very long time. The radio said it happened early in the morning. It would certainly have to have been before ten, because that's when you heard it on the news. You found the thing in your car about — what? — one?" Abby nodded. "So sometime between, say, five and one, somebody killed Jack Pitt and planted something incriminating in your car." *I haven't spilled the beans about the ponytail.* Juss felt very virtuous. *DW would be so proud of me.* A more realistic voice said *You know better,* but her virtuous voice replied *Shut up.*

"You went out that morning," Kerry said. "After you first called me."

"But before that," Greta said. "Did you look out of your window before that and see anybody on the street near your car? Hear anybody driving or walking by who stopped and went on? Hear a car door slam close by?"

91

Abby shook her head, picking at her sandwich. "I wasn't paying any attention. I didn't know I was going to have to."

"Well, sure," Juss said. "How could you know?"

Abby's look of gratitude hurt Juss. *A person shouldn't be grateful because you didn't kick her. No wonder Kerry and Schatzi wrap her in cotton wool.*

"So," Juss said, "you saw the story on the news and it upset you and you called Kerry. And he said to go to a coffee shop. You went?"

"Yes. The CT 'Scape." She pronounced it *cityscape*. "It's on Blankenbaker Avenue, near the Boojum Gallery of Local Art."

Juss laughed. "Oh, yeah — the Boojum! Back in the day, everybody took their stuff to the Boojum." She had thought they were so brave, facing the Boojum with only their art to protect them. Lewis Carroll's "The Hunting of the Snark" with its ominous last line, "For the Snark *was* a Boojum, you see," had harrowed her four-year-old soul, especially the way Moonman had intoned it when he read it to her.

Wonder where Moonman is now, and if he has a real-world name? Wonder where they all are? They had all split without knowing where they were going, and not even Doris knew who or where they were. *Bereft.* Juss felt bereft.

Back to business. "So you went to the CT 'Scape. Did you walk?"

"No, it's too far. I drove. But I didn't pay any attention to the back seat. I didn't open either of the doors on that side of the car. I didn't open either of the back doors. I got in the driver's seat and . . . drove."

Greta said, "Where did you park? On the street? In front of the building, or on a side street?"

"They have a parking lot on the side."

"Windows?" Juss asked. "Could you see your car?"

"Yes, windows. I could see the car when I first came in, but not from the counter. I sat near a window, but my back was to where the car was. I didn't want to see it. Looking at it makes me think about that accident. I didn't hear the door open. I might have heard it, even that far away and through the window. It makes a noise, when you open it. A bad noise."

Kerry's face as he regarded his cousin told Juss that Abby's life was now divided into Before Accident and After Accident.

Juss wrote *No view of car from coffee house.* "And you didn't see anybody from the case pull into the parking lot or go past the parking lot or see you sitting there?"

Abby shook her head mournfully.

Juss wrote *Saw no suspects.* She felt vaguely irritated. Somewhere in here, the falsely accused heroine was supposed to remember a detail she had thought was unimportant, and the clever sleuth was supposed to be like *Aha!*

Suppressing her disappointment, she said, "Then you drove back home, but, again, you didn't have any reason to look in the back seat?"

"Right."

"Did you go straight home? You didn't stop anywhere along the way?"

"No. I went to the 'Scape and then home, and I went right into the house. I was in there about, oh, twenty minutes, getting my library books together. I couldn't find one of them and I went down and opened the back seat door, and. . . ."

Abby's eyes widened and she looked around the table. "It was his hair," she said.

"I beg your pardon?" Kerry said.

"The rat with a red collar. It was his hair." Abby put a hand over her mouth as if she had realized it was his finger or his nose.

So much for my keeping a secret. I might as well have blabbed.

Abby said, "You remember, Kerry. He had that stupid ponytail."

"*Kerry* was in court?"

"Naturally," Kerry said.

"Why didn't you ever say so?"

"I thought it went without saying. Besides, this isn't about me, and there's nothing I can add to what Abby's said. If there had been, I would have."

Juss said, "Witnesses. Did either side call witnesses?"

"Oh, yes," Kerry said. "That was one reason it was so outrageous that Jack Pitt took the case into court. Two men carpooling saw the whole thing and came forward to swear that Marsha Knowles was in the wrong. Pitt made them come in again and again, but they stuck to it."

"What are their names?"

Kerry had to think, but Abby answered, "Mark McGuire and Jeremy Craft. I don't know where they live, but they both work at Like-a-Pro Sporting Goods in the Blankenbaker Mall."

Juss wrote their names and workplace on the suspect list paper in her careful script.

"There's your assignment," she told Kerry, "if you choose to accept it."

"What?"

"Go talk to Abby's witnesses or, better yet, people who know them."

Kerry put down the tea he had been about to drink and said, "You think two carpoolers went in together to run a man down because they had to come to court voluntarily?"

Exasperated, she couldn't even make a coherent gesture.

"No stone unturned," Greta said. "You never know, eh?"

Unsure whether Greta was supporting her or teasing her, she decided to take her at face value.

Witnesses. "Did Marsha Knowles or Jack Pitt have any witnesses?"

Again, Abby answered. "She had a repair estimate from a body shop — It was a funny name, Kerry; do you remember what it was?"

"The Car-O-Practor."

Greta snorted.

Juss wrote down the name. "What was the address?"

"I don't remember."

Juss said, "I'll look it up. Anything else?"

Kerry and Abby shook their heads. Nothing else.

Juss offered everybody more sandwiches, more pickles, more chips, more soda/coffee/tea/water, but lunch was over.

Greta would take Abby home with her, Kerry would begin cataloging the library, and what would she, herself, do? Highgate Commons lurked at the back of her mind like a monster in the closet. She cocked her metaphorical hat, set her metaphorical shoulders, and spit in Highgate Commons' metaphorical eye.

No time like the present. If she waited until Doris got home, Doris would probably throw cold water on the whole project, or at least try to talk her out of visiting the Commons. She felt oddly calm at the prospect of going back, and wondered if it were maturity or repression. *One way to find out.*

As Kerry opened the front door, Abby threw her arms around Juss' neck and hugged her. "Thank you. Thank you for everything."

Juss hugged back, warmed through.

She was warmed even more thoroughly when Greta extended a hand for a farewell shake, smiled, and said, "Call me Schatzi."

Chapter 18

Schatzi checked the dashboard clock. *Plenty of time before the kids get home.*

"Do you feel up to a trip to the library? We could swing by our house and get your books. You never got to go yesterday, what with one thing and another."

Abby shivered slightly. "Yes, I'd like to go to the library. I never did find *The Art of Maxfield Parrish*, though. It's probably in my apartment somewhere. But I'm not sure I want to go back there. It's all right if I stay with you and Kerry for another day or two, isn't it? Just until Saturday?"

"Certainly. Why Saturday?"

"I don't know. Is that too long?"

"No, of course not."

After a moment's silence, Abby said, "Saturday is a nice day. It's a day to stay home and relax, or take a walk or loaf around in your pajamas watching cartoons. It isn't a day you ought to be at work but aren't."

"You'd be happier if you had a job."

"I had a job." Abby looked dark and sullen, as she always did when she talked about the accident and the wreck it had made of her life.

"And now you don't. And the reason is. . . ."

"That bitch and her lies."

"No, the reason is. . . ."

Abby crossed her arms like a petulant child and stared out her side window, finally saying, "I was driving uninsured."

"Yes, you're a very wicked girl and the angels weep for you."

Abby wiped wetness from her cheeks. "I could ask Mr. Delaney to make them give me back my job."

"Do you want to work with them now, after they let you down when you needed them?"

". . . No. Not really."

"You want a new job. Maybe a different job. When we get home from the library, we'll make some lists."

"What kind of lists?" Abby was twisted in her seat to face her now. Schatzi was a watch-the-road driver, but she glanced at her passenger, satisfied to see animation and curiosity instead of defeat.

"Oh, what kind of things you like to do. What kind of jobs you think you would be good at. Skills. Education. Training. Experience. And we'll look in the paper and online."

"I feel bad, taking you away from your work."

Schatzi flapped a dismissive hand. "I checked my email before I came out. All my sites are up-to-date and I can't do anything for the new client until he decides what he wants his site to do. We'll enjoy the afternoon and work this evening. Sound good?"

"Sounds good."

~*~

"I'll meet you here when we're both done," Schatzi said, pointing to a reading alcove near the front desk.

"When?"

Schatzi shrugged. "When we're both done. We'll have

to leave by three at the latest, to be home before the kids get off the bus."

"Okay. . . ." Abby's eyes shifted, and she twisted a lock of her own hair around a finger.

"Abby, did I *ever* forget I had you with me? Did I *ever* go off and leave you? Did *anybody*?"

Abby chuckled and shook her head. "I never thought you would."

No, but you felt it. It must be hell, being you. "Here, let's trade library cards. Now you *know* I won't forget we're together."

Color blotching her cheeks, Abby said, "I know you won't forget."

Schatzi tucked a fluff of Abby's hair behind the younger woman's ear and said, "Good. Because you should know I couldn't forget such an important person."

Abby rolled her eyes — Schatzi watched in fascination; Abby was the only person she had ever seen who actually rolled her eyes in a precise circuit, up, around, and back to where they began — and said, "Im*por*tant?"

"You're important to me and to Kerry and to our children and to all your family and friends. If you don't know that, shame on you. Now go pick out some books. Ones that make you happy."

Leaving Abby was like climbing out of a hot tub full of marshmallows, Schatzi thought with a twinge of guilt.

Vicky is volunteering today. Maybe I can pick up a bit of scuttlebutt on some of these people.

She found Vicky reading the shelves — checking for books that had been put in the wrong place and setting them right.

"Well, look who's here!" Vicky said. "Long time, no see!"

"Are you coming to the next Friends meeting?"

"Lord willin' and the crick don't rise. Did you just stop in to visit, or can I help you find something?"

"I brought Abby to exchange books."

"Her car still not running?"

"Her car is running."

Vicky made a silent movie "surprised" face. "I thought she was in an accident and it was wrecked."

"It was banged up, but it runs."

"I thought I heard it was in the impound lot. I figured it quit on her somewhere and she walked away from it and it got towed before she got back with a tow-truck. Those towing guys are real hot-dogs for impounding your car."

Schatzi clucked in sympathy, showing she remembered when Vicky had had to ransom her own vehicle. "What about the other person's car — the one that hit Abby? Did you hear if it's in the impound lot?"

"No. I guess I just assumed it about Abby's. You know what they say about 'never assume'. I do know the other woman broke a headlight and it crunched her fender up some and knocked the front bumper loose."

"How do you know that?"

Vicky, as she always did when asked that question, winked and tapped the side of her nose and said, "I know Joe." Meaning that she knew a lot of people who knew a lot of things. "I also know that a certain deceased Prosecutor was seen in a dark and romantic restaurant with a certain woman whose car has a broken headlight and a crunched-up fender and a loose front bumper."

"No!"

"Yes! In fact, they were seen more than once. The last time they were in together, they didn't fight or anything — nothing obvious, anyway — but she left with her face turned inside out." Vicky demonstrated by frowning and curving the corners of her mouth down.

"Trouble in Paradise."

"Looked like it. But he was like that. Even in high school, he never appreciated anything he got."

"Did you have him in class?"

"Honey, I started at the high school fresh out of college and I retired from the high school at age 65. I had damn near everybody in the world in class." Vicky moved a book to a lower shelf and straightened the ones left, closing the gap. "If he got a B, he wanted an A. If he got an A, he wanted an A+. He never got an A+. Didn't often get an A. Not an exceptional student. Not nearly as smart as he thought he was. Of course, Einstein wasn't as smart as Jackie Pitt thought *he* was."

Schatzi pulled a book out at random and riffled through it and asked, casually, "Will they miss him much, in the Prosecutor's office?"

"Not so much. He pulled his own weight with the case load, but he creeped so many women out. . . ."

"Ones who worked there?"

"And ones who came in for whatever. That man could give you a hearty handshake and you'd go away thinking you'd been felt up. It was just a way he had. Like a habit. Some women liked it."

Schatzi gave her a gentle nudge with her elbow and a wicked grin. "Did *you* like it?"

"Heh! At my age, I take it where I can get it."

"Did anybody *not* like it? I mean *really* not like it? I don't think I would like it, and I don't think Kerry would like it if I told him about it."

"Oh, everybody knew how Jackie was. Besides, he's gone now, poor boy. Whoever hit him and drove off ought to be ashamed. I guess they were afraid, even not knowing who they hit."

"You think they didn't know?"

"It was early in the morning, he was in his running clothes — nobody looks the same in different clothes and in bad light. Somebody lost control of the car — maybe a student driver or somebody too old to be driving, maybe somebody on dope or sleepy or something, hit somebody and got scared and drove off. They'll turn theirself in by the end of the week, mark my words."

Vicky turned to library politics, and Schatzi had nothing to contribute but the occasional *Oh?* and *No!* and *Really?*

Chapter 19

Juss went into the office and looked up Paul and Genevieve DeSalvo, the renters at Highgate Commons.

After two rings, a light female voice answered, with a slight Hispanic accent, "Hello, this is the DeSalvo residence."

"Hi, Beatriz. This is Juss. Paul or Genny at home?"

"Genny's here. Would you like to speak to her?"

"Yes, please."

She heard Beatriz' soft-soled shoes squeaking on the hardwood floor, then the murmur of voices, and Genny DeSalvo came on.

After exchanging the usual pleasantries, Juss said, "We haven't had a chat for a long time. I was thinking about your garden and wishing I could see it. You still have all those roses?"

"I do. If you have time, you might as well drive out and we'll have coffee on the terrace and I'll give you the grand tour."

"I'd love to. Is now a good time?"

"The sooner the better. I'll have Beatriz whip up some mousse. I believe chocolate is your favorite, isn't it?"

"By name and by nature," Juss said, and held the phone away from her ear while Genny barked a laugh.

She pulled on a suede jacket and got her purse and keys from the office.

"Pray for me, Kerry, I'm off to the rich people's ghetto."

"Now? Don't you have some life coaching to do?"

"Ah, that's the beauty part. They do all the work, and I cash the checks. I have five clients right now, and each of them has an assignment. I'll give them calls tonight to see how they're doing, see if there's anything else they need to succeed at the goals *they set themselves*." She warmed, thinking about the five. Two she liked very much, two she liked well enough and one she liked not at all. But they were all hers — her chicks. *Life is good.*

"If the phone rings, let the machine get it. Let's trade cell phone numbers, in case we need to call each other. — Thanks. — If Doris gets back before I do, tell her I went out and I'll be back for supper."

"All right. —Oh, clock me in before you leave, if you would."

"I clocked you in this morning."

Kerry frowned. "But—"

"But me no buts. Get to work, ya slacker."

His mini-grin told her she was right in thinking he would take the joke.

What a great day this has been, and it's only half over.

~*~

Juss hadn't been to the Commons in years. The renters paid on time or a little bit early, the caretaker did a great job, reported his hours, dropped in at Spadena Street to discuss improvements, and that was that.

The last time she and Doris had gone, to see a two-story addition the caretaker had put up and was justly proud of, she had gone with a stomach ache and had been violently ill when she got back. The time before, it was a headache and the time before, asthma. This time, her stomach didn't

104

hurt, her head didn't hurt — nothing hurt. In fact, she felt like singing.

The song was a childhood gift from her "wastrel hippie" mother before her departure, sung to a tune from an obscure musical:

I'm Injustice H. Choc'lit
If you think that's weird, you're boring!
Boo, Injustice! Yay, Choc'lit!
Now you know about my name.

It was difficult to sort out her feelings toward her parents. They had left her at the commune, certain it — and she — would be there whenever they returned, although they could have found her through Grannie Ruth, if they had ever come back. After all, everybody raised all the kids, so it wasn't as though she had been abandoned. Not exactly. They had left her, expecting she would be raised in a loving environment where her needs would be met and her name would not be a burden.

Free spirits Harold (Mandrake) Madison and Bridget (Pacific) Haggarty had believed in balance. When it came to naming their child, their idea of balance had been to name her after something bad and something good, with a blend of their own discarded "establishment" names in the center. It could have been, she had come to realize, worse. Boogers Madhag Orgasm, for example. Injustice H. Chocolate was practically normal.

After the commune broke up and she and Doris had moved into an apartment, public elementary school had been a shock, but not too bad. Other kids had names like Rudolph and Olive that they would love as adults but hated as children. And Chocolate was a name every kid envied.

Seventh and eighth grades, though, had been hell. Again, she wasn't alone in that — seventh and eighth grades, she had learned later, were hell for most people. At the time, though, part of the torment is the firm belief that you're the only one in the world being targeted by the bullies and the snobs. Money was no armor, family was no defense — if you had that "kick me" sign on your butt, nothing could cover it up or make it go away.

She had almost given up pacifism once or twice a week.

Doris had gotten her through it, and high school had been better. Well, it had to be, didn't it?

She pulled into the Highgate Commons drive and through the open gate which would be locked at eleven and unlocked at eight.

All the houses were set well back from the curving road, atop sloping lawns or landscaped terraces. Each house was unique — this wasn't suburbia, after all — and, Juss had to admit, delightfully interesting. Great-grandmama's old pad was built of honey-colored stone with a deep porch across the front, the porch roof held up by red columns — probably carved out of solid blocks of semi-precious stone. *Ha!* It made Juss want to spit.

She drove up and parked on the double-car-width loop that circled the fountain in front of the house, wishing she drove a heap instead of a well-kept Mini-Cooper.

But it wasn't fair to take Great-grandmama out on the DeSalvos.

Beatriz, a pale young woman with rosy cheeks and chestnut hair, opened the door with a smile on her round face.

"Good to see you again, Juss."

"Hi, Beatriz. How's it going?"

"Oh, it's going great!" She led Juss down a long hall into a white-carpeted living room and through sliding glass doors onto a shaded terrace. "My brother flew back to El Salvador yesterday. He had a great vacation, but he felt guilty being away from his patients. He was calling them on his cell phone and talking to the office all the time." She laughed, showing dimples. "He wants me to join him after I get my nursing degree, but I'm an American now, you know?"

Genny DeSalvo turned from a flower box, a heavy cut-glass vase half-full of water in her right hand, a rainbow of marigolds in the other. She was dressed in casual clothes that probably cost as much as a week's salary for Beatriz, but had probably been bought twenty years ago. Her hair was cut very short and dyed a quite natural-looking blond.

"I hope you don't mind marigolds," she said. "Some people don't care for the scent, but I think they look and smell divine. I grow these in the hothouse, so I'll have them all year." She put the vase on the glass top of the patio table.

"They're very pretty." *And very stinky.* "Thanks for having me over."

"Oh, you're welcome! Let's have our tour and then our refreshments. Is that all right? Coffee or tea? Hot or cold?"

"Hot coffee, if it's made."

"Two, please, Beatriz. And the mousse, when it's ready."

"Sure."

Genny fussed with the flowers, avoiding Juss' eyes.

When she looked up and said, "Shall we?" and gestured toward the patio steps, she was looking at the garden, not at Juss.

Juss trailed her along the paths and through the hothouse, admiring the marigolds and roses, the hostas and ferns, the hardy in-season and the cosseted out-of-season. She admired the small kitchen garden Beatriz maintained, thinking smugly of how much bigger and more varied the one at home was.

When they had settled into the padded chairs beside the round patio table, Genny gave a forced laugh and said,

"All right. Go on and give me the bad news."

"What bad news?"

"It's about the house, isn't it? If you're raising the rent, we understand. Paul and I have been expecting it, with the housing shortage what it is and so many executives moving to the outlying towns to get away from the city crime and pollution. We knew this house at this price was too good to last. All we ask is that, if you've decided to sell it, you give us the chance to meet any price you're offered."

Well, of all the— "My gosh, Genny, if I had to raise the rent, I'd raise the rent; I wouldn't act like I wanted to visit and then blind-side you. And I would never sell the house out from under you."

Genny barked another weak laugh. "Business is business, after all."

"I *do* business. I don't *give* people the business."

Beatriz brought out a tray and each took a china cup and saucer, a yellow linen napkin and a crystal bowl of fluffy chocolate with a silver spoon sticking out of it. Genny lifted a silver coffee pot off the tray and poured coffee for them both, putting the pot within easy reach.

They thanked Beatriz, and she went back inside.

"I'm sorry if I offended you," Genny said. "But I've grown very attached to this house, especially the garden."

"I can see why you would. It's beautiful."

"Paul and I have often wondered if you might not want the house for yourself at some point."

This house? Live in this *house?*

In a way, the idea had a certain evil appeal. She could imagine dancing through the rooms, singing, "Spinning, spinning in your graaaave like a top!" But that would be mean.

"No, I like where I'm living now."

"It is a precious little house."

"Yes, it is. Yes, it is."

"This is purely a social visit, then?"

Crossing her fingers under the table, Juss said, "Sure. I wanted to see how things are going here. Catch up with the gossip."

Genny's eyes sparkled. In another income bracket, she'd be leaning over the back fence to dish the dirt.

Juss listened with feigned interest to the problems and suspected problems afflicting the affluent. The prices were higher but the vices were the same here as on Spadena Street or anywhere. Well, most places wouldn't get up a neighborhood petition against the grass somebody chose for his front lawn or threaten to serve papers if you put up multi-colored Christmas lights instead of white ones, but *mostly* they were the same.

At last, patience paid off.

"And then there's Marsha Knowles. That little girl is *looking* for trouble, if you ask me."

"Where does she live?"

Genny wove a route through the air with a manicured nail. "If you follow the road past us, you pass the Baumhardts' with the terraced flowerbeds out front? You know? Have you been up that far? They have banana plants and ferns and all the creeping phlox?"

"Oh, yes." Doris had driven her past, the last time they had come out. Doris had a real weakness for ground cover.

"Well, her house is the next one. It's the smallest one in the Commons, but she keeps it well."

"So what about her?"

"She was in court. *Traffic* court."

"No!"

"Yes! More coffee?"

"Thanks."

As she poured, Genny said, "She was in an accident. Somebody plowed into her — *she* says — but we've all seen how she drives around here."

"Reckless?"

"Careless. You'd better look out, because it's *her* road. And if she'll drive that way here, I can only imagine how she must drive out there. However, the story is that she was hit, and the Prosecutor begged her to come to court and put the man behind bars."

"It was a man?" If Marsha had a history of false claims. . . .

Genny shrugged. "Oh, I don't know. I assumed it was a man, but it does seem as if I heard it was a woman. A sales clerk or something, maybe. Anyway, she went to court, and she lost."

The word *lost* was said with great relish.

"Was she upset?"

"I would think so. But the worst thing is, she hasn't had her car repaired yet."

"Oh? Wonder why not."

"Well, she couldn't, could she, as long as the case was active? She had to show the damage, in case the judge or the jury or whatever wanted to see it. She had the repair estimated, but she didn't have the work done."

"Oh, yes. Of course."

"But the case is over, and she still hasn't had the car repaired. Every day, we have to look at that rattletrap coming and going."

"Maybe she can't afford the repairs."

Genny looked askance. "Please. If she can't afford car repairs, she couldn't afford to live here."

"What was I thinking?"

"Would you like some more mousse?"

"No, thank you. It's very good, though."

"I'm so glad you like it."

"Beatriz is a fantastic cook."

"She is." The appreciation on Genny's face reminded Juss of why she liked her. A person couldn't help being born rich — couldn't help thinking lots of money was normal. People usually thought the way things were when they were growing up was the "real" way. But some people thought any other way was bad and some people thought any other way was only different. Genny and Paul were "different" people, not "bad" people. *And all Rich people aren't "bad" just because Great-grandmama was a condescending snob.*

Juss said, "I take it you don't like this traffic court lady very much."

"Marsha Knowles? Not many people here like her very much. She ignores the Planning and Zoning regulations unless she's forced to comply. She never contributes to community fund raising."

"Doesn't she have any friends in the Commons? That's kind of sad."

"I think she gets along well enough with Priscilla Bingly. That's her neighbor on the other side of Jonathan's — Jonathan Prescott's is the place with the gorgeous landscaping, this side of Marsha's."

"That's something. Assuming Priscilla is all right."

"Priscilla's a darling. Anybody who couldn't get along with Priscilla would be simply *impossible*."

"Does Priscilla work outside the home?" Juss asked.

"Yes, poor thing. Benjamin didn't leave her very well provided for. But she knew somebody who knew somebody who got her a job as receptionist at the public radio station." She leaned forward, eyes twinkling at the surprise she was about to share. "The *jazz* one."

Juss wasn't certain how she was expected to respond, so she chuckled, and that seemed to work. "Well, I mustn't keep you from your garden. Thank you so much for the visit and the tour, and I'm sorry I worried you about the house."

"Don't think a thing of it. I love it so, here."

Genny linked arms with her and walked her to the front door.

"Don't be such a stranger," Genny said. "Come again, when Paul can see you. I know he'd love to."

"Well, thank you." *I might come, if you ever actually invited me.*

Halfway to the car, her cellphone rang. It was one of

her clients, calling her personal number because it was a perceived emergency.

Might as well go on and put this fire out. The only thing I got here was a snack. That, and the end of Great-grandmama's curse.

Chapter 20

Juss dragged in at 5:30, not surprised to see Kerry's green VW gone, and not entirely sorry. Her fizzy idea of finding Pitt's killer and freeing Abby of suspicion and worry seemed silly now. Her client had been calling from the hospital, having had her nose broken by The Daughter-In-Law From Hell. The client's son was rationalizing the attack, and the client felt like she was having a psychotic break over it. Oh, no, no, no police! Juss had finally connected the client with a family counselor who would deal with single members of troubled families, if that single member was the only one who would come in.

"Girl, you look beat," Doris said from the kitchen. "Come in here and take your medicine and I'll get supper finished."

Juss sat down before her "medicine" — a glass of red wine and a piece of 70% cacao dark chocolate — and let the tension drain away.

"What you been up to today?" Doris asked.

"Worked on an actual real problem for a client. What time did Kerry leave?"

"Five o'clock, on the dot. I signed him out."

Juss, her mouth busy with chocolate, nodded.

After looking at Juss silently for a moment, Doris said, "That boy sure is a worker. He doesn't take anything for granted, either. You know that appraisal that the appraiser your great-grandma had appraise the books left?"

"Oh, gosh, I forgot all about it."

"I showed it to Kerry and he right away saw that it only appraised the hardbacks, and only some of them. Remember how Granny Ruth used to say that some of the books were her mother's and some were her father's and all the paperbacks were her husband's and none of them were hers? I bet anything the books that didn't get appraised were your great-grandpa's and your grandpa's."

"So if Kerry separates the appraised books from the others, I would have my great-grandpa's and my grandpa's libraries?"

"Right."

Juss had never known her great-grandfather or her grandfather. They had died before she had been retrieved from communal hippiedom. Now, she would have a chance to get to know them, through their choices of books. That made those books valuable beyond price.

Happy!

She asked Doris about her day at the clothes closet while they ate supper. Over the dishes, Juss confessed the after-court war council and the assignments they had all taken on.

"You better leave those people alone," Doris said. "You better stay out of police business. You mess things up for them, how is that going to be good for Abby?"

Juss couldn't object. "It seems kind of harebrained now."

Doris gave her a quick, one-armed hug. "It was a sweet thought, to help that girl. You always were the helpingest child."

When the dishes were done, Juss went to the office and played back the three messages on her answering machine.

One was from her client of the afternoon, thanking her. The other two were from other clients, reporting on their progress. She pulled up their case files and made entries. She played with some personal email and visited some websites and blogs she enjoyed. At a quarter to eight, Doris called to her from the living room.

"You want to come see what Kerry's been doing before our shows come on?"

One of the side tables was stacked with books — paperbacks and shabby hardbacks.

"Oh, not this one!" Juss picked up a small volume with the paper on its stitched spine missing.

"Don't have a conniption, that isn't going anywhere. He says that's the repair stack."

"Okay." Juss stroked the scarred and grubby cover with its depiction of the happy Cratchit family on the front and a reformed Scrooge smiling on the back. She opened the front cover. The pages were yellowed and some had small rips. The flyleaf was inscribed, in a childish scrawl, *Genarose Leister, 3B, J. B. Atkinson School.* She didn't know Genarose Leister and there was no J. B. Atkinson School in Jorisburg. She had bought the book at a yard sale when she was seven, and she had read it every Christmas since, wondering who Genarose Leister was and what her life was like.

"Where are the ones beyond repair?" she asked.

Doris chuckled. "There isn't one. The boy's like you — the more raggedy a book is, the more he wants to save it."

Juss, gratified at having made such a perfect hire, put the old book back on the stack.

The doorbell rang.

Doris and Juss exchanged *You expecting anybody?* glances.

Doris lifted a foot, displaying her favorite, rundown house slippers.

Juss chuckled and said, "I'll get it."

When she opened the door, she was delighted to see her neighborhood client, Chickapoo Tomaneck, holding a foil-wrapped rectangle.

Lava cake!

She was far less delighted to see two vaguely familiar women, one around her own age, one around half that, on the bricks below the steps.

When she looked to her client for explanation, Mrs. Tomaneck made such an eloquent series of facial expressions, Juss wanted to applaud and cry, "Do it again!"

With twitches, grimaces, and eyerolls, Mrs. Tomaneck managed to convey, *These women attached themselves to me and I have to pretend it's okay, but I would never have brought them on my own and watch out for them.*

It was an impressive performance.

"Come in, Mrs. Tomaneck, and welcome," Juss said. "Who are your friends?"

The slight stiffening of the two women's expressions told Juss they were aware of her implication that they were *not* welcome. She appreciated Mrs. Tomaneck's warning.

"Oh," Mrs. Tomaneck said, handing Juss the rectangle, "watch out for this — it's still warm. I made you and Doris your own little lava cake, so the goosh would goosh out when you cut it, just like a big one. That's part of the fun, I always think."

The women on the bricks exchanged superior smirks, then turned innocent eyes to Juss.

Mrs. Tomaneck gestured toward them. "This is Mamie Adagio and Florence Adagio, her sister-in-law. Mamie and her husband live next door to me. They asked me where I was going with this lava cake and I told them and they wanted to come along."

She made some more faces, indicating, *Seriously. Watch out.*

The women looked at each other again, as if they were both shy, and the younger one said, "You tell her, Mamie, dear."

"It's really your idea, sweetheart, but, oh, well. . . ." With a little laugh that wanted to be silvery, Mamie said, "We need to consult you about a business matter."

"Oh, I'm so sorry," Juss said, as if she were. "I don't do business consulting. I'm a Life Coach. I only consult on personal matters."

The young woman gave the older one a tiny push on the shoulder with her fingertips. "I told you."

The older woman blessed the younger one with a smile that could etch glass and said, "Oh, but Miss . . . *Chocolate* . . . our business is so small." She held two fingers almost touching. "Soooo small. It might even be smaller than yours."

Zing!

"I wish I could help, but I'm not qualified to give business advice."

The younger woman smiled sweetly and said, "But you are qualified to give personal advice?"

Zing!

"Yes," said Juss. "I am."

The older woman gave her silverish laugh again and said, "If we ever need any personal advice, then, we'll bear you in mind. Won't we, Florence?"

"Oh," said Florence, "we certainly will."

"I hope so," Juss lied. "Although I can't imagine either of you charming people ever needing personal advice."

They simpered at each other, clearly signaling, to one on the look-out, that neither thought *she* needed personal advice, but that the *other* could definitely use some.

The older one said, "We'll be running along, then. We'll have to come to some decision all on our lonesome. Come on, Chickie; we'll walk you home."

"You go on," Mrs. Tomaneck said. "I want to say hey to Doris. G'night!" She stepped in and closed the door. Then she puffed air up over her forehead.

At the same time, Doris came into the entry. When she saw company, she almost ducked back, but came out to give Mrs. Tomaneck a hug when she saw who it was.

"Long time closing that door," she said.

"Juss was showing those Adagio women how it's done," Mrs. Tomaneck said.

Juss gave a shudder that was only slightly exaggerated. "Did I?"

"You let them know you knew they were talking out of both sides of their mouths, and you did enough of it yourself to let them know you knew how, too. And you did it without getting ugly, which is more than most of us on the street can do. The rest of us either don't see it or can't do it or end up snarling at them."

Doris and Chickapoo chorused, "Couple of vipers," and laughed at the echo.

Mrs. Tomaneck said, "I came in to tell Juss I talked

to Bee-Beep like she said, and he's tickled pink about me working and doing so well. He says he brags about me at the barber shop and all his friends are jealous."

Bright spots of color bloomed on her cheeks as she said this, making her look more like an Easter basket chick than ever.

She nodded at the rectangle Juss held. "I brought my payment."

Doris said, "I don't know what you're talking about, but if that's what it smells like it is, I don't care."

Mrs. Tomaneck clapped a hand over her mouth, eyes rounded into circles. "I forgot about the privilege!"

Trying not to laugh, Juss said, "If you mean coach/client privilege, that means *I'm* not allowed to tell, not you."

"Okay. So I can tell? Yes? Well, I came last night and asked your Juss for some advice, and she was brilliant, just wonderful, and I did what she said and it worked like a charm. And all she charged me was some lava cake. Wasn't that sweet?"

"It was," said Doris, with a smile that warmed Juss to her toes. "That was real sweet of her. Come on in and have some with us."

"No, I need to run on. Those Adagios are probably waiting to clock how long I stay. I was hoping you'd warned Juss about them, and it looks like you did."

"I didn't. I didn't expect her to run into them. She's just canny."

"Well, no wonder she's so good at what she does." Mrs. Tomaneck gave Juss's wrist a friendly squeeze. "And did I say to call me Chickapoo? Call me Chickapoo. 'Kay?"

"Okay."

Happy!

~*~

The lava cake was warm and gooshy.

As they ate it, Juss said, "Why didn't you tell me Chickapoo Tomaneck was so cute? And why didn't you warn me about those Adagio vipers?"

Doris licked chocolate lava off her spoon and said, "You never wanted to hear anything about the neighborhood. So I stopped trying to tell you anything about it."

Juss felt herself flush. It was true. *Tourists*, she had called her neighbors. As if *they* were the ones coming in from outside.

"So," she said, putting an extra spoon of lava over Doris' cake, "tell me."

Chapter 21

Kerry backed out of the driveway into the street, lowered the window long enough to wave goodbye to the children over the top of the car, and drove away.

Schatzi waved until she couldn't see the little hands and faces anymore.

"I think Mom and Dad were disappointed that Abby was watching the kids tonight," she said.

"When they moved into the duplex, I told them we wouldn't take advantage of them. They were not to be afraid we'd consider them built-in babysitters. I believe we've kept our word on that."

"I believe we have, and I believe they appreciate it, but I think they were *disapPOINted toNIGHT.*"

"Perhaps. If so, I doubt Abby will be alone with her task. We'll probably come home to find all six of them crammed onto the couch watching *Just Visiting* or *Spaced Invaders.*"

He sensed Schatzi looking at him.

"I'm not saying there's anything wrong with that," he said, "although if I hear about the mean girl falling off the desk or the little boy dressed like a duck many more times, my ears may shrivel closed in self-defense."

"No, you'll have to endure it. Smug people's ears never shrivel closed."

"Smug? I?"

She tugged the lobe of his nearer ear and said, "A little. Now and then. Just around the edges."

He hated it when they quarreled, but he wasn't quite finished being offended.

"Were you not smug when you came home from the library and reported that Vicky's gossip was faulty?"

"How often is Vicky Basinger wrong? I can't believe the police have such tight control of this that Vicky doesn't know about something being found in the back of Abby's car. You still haven't forgiven her for catching you passing a note to Freddy Pollen in assembly, you scofflaw."

He was happy to laugh and end the dissension. "The woman is part bloodhound. But now we can tell Old Lady Basinger—" he sang the national childhood anthem, "*we know some-thing you don't know.*"

"Together, you and I are going to uncover subtle clues that the baffled police force missed and bring a criminal to justice. He's a librarian. She designs web sites. Together, they fight crime."

"And don't forget Juss."

"Oh, no, how could I? That's the title of our show — *Angels of Injustice*. Do you like it?"

"Love it! And you would be played by Keira Knightly."

"Who would play you?"

"Orlando Bloom, of course."

"Who would play Juss?"

"Johnny Depp?"

Schatzi laughed until she cried.

~*~

As he held the mall door for her, Kerry asked, "Split up, or come with me to the sporting goods store?"

"I'll come with you. We can probably actually get something for Joel there."

Like-a-Pro was the anchor store, a two-story big-box all in itself with the rest of the Mall running like a hall in front of it.

Kerry and Schatzi walked into the store arm-in-arm, a little overwhelmed by the sheer magnitude of its offerings.

"Dear God," Kerry said, "it's like stepping onto the holodeck in Star Trek. Look — isn't that Captain Picard?"

"Stop teasing me; it's cruel."

A slightly plump man with a steel-gray crewcut and a name badge that read *Brad* came smiling up to them.

"Evening, folks. What can I do you for?"

"We're . . . er . . . looking for something for our son's eleventh birthday."

"Sure! What's he into? Hunting, fishing, skateboarding, skiing, mountain bikes, football. . . ?"

"Hiking," Schatzi said.

"Hiking?" This was the first Kerry knew of it.

"And camping out."

"Hiking and camping out?"

Brad laughed and wagged a finger. "Ah, momma knows. Sure, folks; right this way to our hiking and camping section."

"When did he become interested in hiking and camping out?" Kerry whispered.

"Since he made friends with Eddie Laughton," Schatzi whispered back. "Eddie invited him to a campout in the Forestry, and he said he couldn't go because he didn't have any equipment."

"Why didn't he tell me?"

"I told him to put it on his Christmas list. So now

he won't be expecting it for his birthday, and he'll be surprised."

"Here we are!" Brad said. "You folks want to look around, or do you need a little guidance?"

"Two boys camping in the Forestry," Kerry said. "That doesn't sound safe, to me."

"I didn't mean only the two of them. Eddie's parents and his two older brothers — or sisters — or one of each — I forget — will be along, too. They do it all the time."

"I don't know. . . ."

To Brad, Schatzi said, "We need to look at a one-boy tent, a sleeping bag, a canteen, a backpack, and a lantern. And a good book for an eleven-year-old on camping techniques and safety."

"Good quality," Kerry said, "but not too expensive. After all," he told Schatzi, "he might not like it, and then what would we do with all that equipment?"

The happy salesman rattled away to himself, comparing the points of this product and the drawbacks of that one, the value-for-money of this tent and that. When he paused to check the price of a lantern, Kerry asked, "Mark McGuire and Jeremy Craft work here, don't they?"

"Sure. Why?"

"Not that you aren't doing an excellent job. I'm sure they couldn't be better."

"Well, you know, they might be better. I'm more of a football man, myself, but they both love to hike and camp."

"Are they here?"

"No, they work the day shift."

"Never mind, then."

"Where did you meet Jeremy and Mark?"

Schatzi said, "At the courthouse."

"Oh, yeah, that. I had to come in and cover for both of them twice over that. Pulled split shifts — That's a bear, you know?"

"Yes." Schatzi did her Mother Hen cluck and Kerry watched in fascination as the man with the steel-colored crewcut told mamma all about it.

"It wasn't their fault, I guess. I blame the justice system. I mean, aren't there any real criminals around, that they have to go after a fender bender? It's not like anybody died or anything. They shouldn't have got involved. It wasn't anything to do with them."

Schatzi raised an eyebrow, and Brad back-pedaled.

"I mean, they did the right thing, coming forward and doing their civic duty and that. Those little gals in their jazzy cars, driving like maniacs — not that I think women drivers are automatically bad drivers, I don't mean that. But that one was. So I guess she ought to be taught a lesson. But it sure made it hard on me." He lowered himself into a camp chair with an umbrella fixed to its frame and gestured to two others facing it. "Try these out. They fold up into nothing. You can keep a couple of them in your trunk for if you go to the beach or the river or a picnic or whatever. So anyway, they're driving along, on their way to work, and this gal in a jazzy car starts weaving in and out of traffic — jumping line, you know? So this other gal pulls out of a side street and starts to turn, and this first gal pops right into her. Pop! So Mark pulls over and calls a cop and waits and they give a statement. So naturally they get called in to make it official. And again and again. And then there's a court date. Well, I

126

can't complain, I guess, I made some extra hours, some extra money, right?"

"Right," Schatzi said. Kerry was glad, because he had rather lost track of the possibility that this might turn into more than a monologue. She said, "I'll bet they were ticked — missing all that work."

"Were they ever! Days when the criminal justice system kindly allowed them to work, our shifts overlap by a half an hour and I'd get a earful! If words could kill!"

"I can't say I blame them," Schatzi said. "That prosecutor should be ashamed of himself."

"Too late! Didn't you hear? Got himself bumped off in a hit-and-run. But no, he's not the one they were ticked with — it was that lying little gal in the jazzy car and that goof-ball she hit. Turns out that one was driving without insurance and that's what triggered the whole thing. Oh, they had a few choice words for that Jack Pitt, but it was the gals they blamed for all the lost time."

Kerry was glad to let Schatzi take the lead in choosing a sleeping bag, backpack and essential gear for a tenderfoot camping trip and having them wrapped. He barely listened as Brad and the wrapping desk clerk reminisced for them about camping trips they had taken when they were young. He nodded at the bill and watched her write the check and smiled and shook hands with Brad and insisted on carrying most of the packages but hardly felt present until they were out of the store.

"Schatzi, I laughed when Juss suggested it, but what if these men did run Jack Pitt down? Suppose they happened to see him and recognize him and took the opportunity? The one who was driving, I mean. Or the other one could have grabbed the wheel on impulse and forced the car off the road."

"Oh, they wouldn't have!" After a moment, she said, "But they could have been trying to frighten him, and . . . I don't know . . . stepped on the gas instead of the brake? A Freudian slip?"

"Then they decided to — no pun intended — kill two birds with one stone and implicate Abby."

"Why not the other woman? The 'little gal in the jazzy car'?"

Kerry increased his stride so he could shoulder the door open for Schatzi. Schatzi came through at a run so she could hold the outer door for him before he could get to it.

They navigated the parking lot and stowed the packages in the trunk. Then he said, "How do we know they didn't?"

"You've lost me."

He hardly registered Schatzi holding out her hand for the car keys, but automatically put them in her outstretched palm.

He said, "How do we know the two men didn't implicate the other woman? Marsha Knowles? Nobody seems to know about what they found in Abby's car — if it was, indeed, something that implicated her. It could be that the police found something that implicated Marsha Knowles and are keeping it secret. It could be that she found it first and destroyed it. But, Schatzi. . . ."

They got into the car and Schatzi backed out an inch at a time, forcing the driver who was waiting to pounce on the parking space to back up until there was actually room for her to get out of his way.

When she had enough attention free she said, "I'm listening. 'But, Schatzi' what?"

"What if those men — or one of those men — want to do more than implicate the women? What if they killed Jack Pitt deliberately, and intend to kill the women, too? What if what they left in Abby's car was meant to be a warning?"

Schatzi's hands tightened on the wheel. "But you laughed at the idea."

"Because I was assuming an ordinary mind-set. One or both of them might be unstable. Or the Pitt death may have been, as you say, semi-accidental and now they feel they have nothing more to lose. Schatzi, we have to call the police about this."

When she didn't throw common-sense over him, he knew she agreed, and was chilled.

They rode in silence, Kerry keeping his eyes on Schatzi and Schatzi watching the road. Then she said, "Call that lawyer."

"Mr. Delaney?"

"The one who was at court today. The one Juss hired for Abby. He'll know what's best to do."

Kerry unclenched himself. *Dear girl! Of course!* "You're absolutely right. As soon as we get home, I'll ask Abby for Mr. Delaney's card."

"But don't tell her why. She's safe at our house, even if the worst case is true, and she wouldn't sleep tonight if she thought there were the least danger."

"Right again. I'll tell her I want the card because I'm afraid she'll lose it."

"Now let's hope she hasn't, already."

~*~

The younger children were asleep but Joel still had half an hour of reading in bed before lights out. Mr. and Mrs.

129

Metzenberger, Schatzi's parents, were sitting at the kitchen table with Abby, playing a three-handed game of cards.

"Hello." Schatzi kissed all three on the tops of their heads.

Kerry nodded to them. "What are you playing?"

"Dang if I know," Mr. Metzenberger said. "It started out gin rummy but it can't be gin rummy."

"Why not?"

"Because I always win at gin rummy. I'm the king of gin rummy. And this Abby girl is beating the pants off me. I'm sitting here in my skivvies."

"Frank!" Mrs. Metzenberger pretended to be shocked.

"It's my firm belief she's cheating. I think she's reading the reflection of my cards off my head." He rubbed his bald crown, surrounded by a short chestnut fringe.

Mrs. Metzenberger stacked her cards together and put them face down.

"How did the shopping trip go?"

"Perfect," Schatzi said.

Mr. Metzenberger put a finger to his lips, cocked his head toward Joel's room and pantomimed throwing a baseball and then flipped one ear with a finger, his sign for "Little pitchers have big ears" —children hear everything.

Schatzi nodded and repeated. "It was perfect."

They had left the packages in the trunk. Tomorrow, while the kids were in school, Schatzi would hide Joel's presents in the Metzenbergers' side of the house.

~*~

Abby, for a wonder, had Mr. Delaney's card and gave it to Kerry with an air of passing on a burden.

Kerry and Schatzi kissed Joel goodnight, leaving Abby to read to him from *Percy Jackson and the Olympians*, and retreated to their bedroom, closing the door behind them.

"What if she picks up the extension to make a call while you're still on?" Schatzi asked.

"Ah! That's why I'm going to use my cell phone."

"Clever boy. Give me the card and I'll read the number off to you."

Kerry more than half expected to get an answering machine and hoped he didn't get flustered, dictating such a melodramatic message to a machine, but after a click that signaled call-forwarding, Mr. Delaney answered.

"Mr. Delaney, Schatzi and I were at Like-a-Pro Sporting Goods Store tonight, and the names of Mark McGuire and Jeremy Craft came up when we were talking to the salesman—"

"Oh! That girl!" Mr. Delaney interrupted. "She's dragged you into it, I see. As if she weren't bad enough, now she's cloning herself."

"I beg your pardon. I'm afraid I don't catch your meaning."

"You went out there to talk to the witnesses at Abby's driving uninsured trial, didn't you?"

"Schatzi and I went there to buy birthday presents for our son." *That's why* Schatzi *and I went there.*

"That sounds like Juss-talk for 'Yes, I did, but here's my cover story.' Well, go on. You went out there and what happened?"

"They weren't there, but the salesman we had was more than a little garrulous. The trial came up somehow — he was telling us about working extra hours — he was telling us about a lot of things, to be quite honest. At any rate . . . ." He told Mr. Delaney what Brad had said and what he and Schatzi had talked about in the car and their concern for Abby's and Marsha Knowles' safety.

Mr. Delaney made a non-committal grunt. "It doesn't sound too likely, but it'll muddy the waters, just in case they *are* considering Abby a suspect. I'll call Sheriff Cornflower and put a flea in his ear about it."

"Thank you, Mr. Delaney. Thank you so much."

"Don't let Juss lead you into temptation. No poking around in police business, right?"

"Of course not. Would you like to know what we purchased?"

"I meant no offense, Mr. Dashingly."

"Apology accepted, Mr. Delaney."

There was an extended pause, then Mr. Delaney said, "I'll call Carlton Cornflower now. Give my best to Miss Andrews."

Chapter 22

Juss answered the phone in her office. "IHC Enterprises, how may I help you?"

"Hello," DW's tenor voice said, in its most official smoothness. "May I speak to your brick wall? 'Cause I know you aren't going to listen to me."

"Hi, DW. What'd I do now?" She searched her conscience, but it told her she was innocent. It had fooled her before, so that was no comfort.

"I just got off the phone with Carlton Cornflower. Ask me why."

"Why?"

"Because I got a call from your stooge, Kerry Dashingly."

"My stooge?"

"Your stooge. Your shill. Your catspaw. Your pawn. Whatever you want to call him. He claims he and his wife went to Like-a-Pro tonight to do some shopping, but you know what? While they happened to be shopping where Miss Andrews' witnesses work, the names of those witnesses happened to drop into their conversation with the salesman. Isn't that a coincidence? And the salesman tied them up and forced them to listen to him talk about those witnesses."

"So they want you to sue him for unlawful restraint?"

"Awww. Aren't you the cutest, funniest little thing?"
I hate it when he does that.

"Sarcasm doesn't suit you, DW. You're hurting my feelings. You really are."

"Don't try to put me in the wrong. Juss, you are not to meddle in police business. You are not to put anybody else up to meddling in police business. You understand?"

"Of course I understand! Do you mind telling me what police business is, here? Have I meddled with Mrs. Pitt or Sharon Pitt? No. Has anybody talked to anybody in his office? No." *Not yet.* "Has anybody crossed the police tape and messed around in the crime scene?" *Oooo!* "No. So what are you chewing me out for? Why did Kerry call you, anyway? To tell on me? Is he a stooge or a stool-pigeon?"

"Aw, you've got those poor people so uptight they squeak when they walk. They've cooked it up that those two witnesses are psychopaths and killed Pitt and framed Miss Andrews and might do harm to her and Marsha Knowles, all because they got jerked around by the legal system."

"That's goofy. Isn't it?"

"Probably. That's what I mean. Thinking like that is the result of your getting them keyed up about 'solving the crime', Juss."

"But you called the sheriff."

"Yes. It's an unlikely theory, but — unlike some people — I know enough to make my own decisions about what's important and what should be done or not done. I felt it was my responsibility to pass the possibility on to the person whose job it is to deal with it."

"I appreciate your calling me, but why did you call the sheriff?"

There was a silence that was at once very cold and very hot.

"I'm sorry, DW," Juss said meekly. "I shouldn't have been so smart-mouth. But Abby's scared and Kerry and Schatzi are worried about her. I am, too. We wouldn't bother the widow or Jack Pitt's daughter. That would be mean. But Abby looks like an obvious suspect, and if Carlton Cornflower wastes time investigating her the less obvious leads might dry up. All I'm doing is kind of poking around the corners of things, places that probably won't get looked at. I'm not getting in the way, because nobody's looking where I'm looking or asking what I'm asking."

"You don't know that."

"Nobody yet has said, 'That's what the police asked when they were here.' So."

DW sighed heavily. "Well, Brick Wall, pass my message on to Juss when she comes in. And have her tell Mr. Dashingly I did call Carlton Cornflower and pass on his and Mrs. Dashingly's message."

"Okay."

"Okay?"

"Okay!"

"*Okay.*"

"G'night, DW. Don't be mad."

"Good night, Brick Wall." The tenor voice had softened. "Don't be a thick brick wall." *Click.*

Chapter 23

When Kerry rang the bell at 1 Spadena Street the next morning, Doris answered the door.

"Come on in and have some coffee before you get started. Juss told me to sign you in when you got here, so your time sheet is in the kitchen. Something else is in there, too."

The glitter of anticipated vicarious pleasure radiated so strongly from her, Kerry wanted to ask *Is it a puppy?*

It was his office computer, a slender all-in-one beauty with wireless keyboard and mouse.

"It came last night about seven. Juss fired it up to make sure it worked. She seemed pleased."

It was a beautiful little machine.

"You sure that's gonna be big enough for you?"

"Oh, yes."

"Yes." Doris took one of his hands and examined it. "You got those piano hands. Long skinny fingers to reach all those keys. You play piano?"

"No."

"Maybe you ought to take lessons. Never too late."

She poured them coffee and put napkins and a plate of cookies on the table.

"Did you make these?" Kerry asked.

"Me and Nabisco. Juss is the baker."

"They're very good." Kerry nibbled until he saw Doris dunk hers in her coffee, then he happily followed suit.

"Is she not here?"

"No, she went out. Had some client visits to make. She said to tell you she isn't mad at you for calling DW Delaney. She said you did the right thing."

"I take it he called her?"

Doris nodded. "Called her and tried to jerk a knot in her tail over the phone wire. She don't jerk easy, though." She had that exasperated but nevertheless proud look Mr. Metzenberger got when he was telling about something bewilderingly, creatively wrong the children had done.

"I didn't intend to make trouble for her."

"Oh, she knows that. Like I said, she said you did the right thing. You were worried about your cousin, and even that other woman. You had to tell somebody. If she got in trouble, it was her own doing."

"I didn't have to go along with her ideas."

Doris shrugged and smiled. "Folks do. That's what makes her a good Life Coach." As if reminding herself she disapproved, she said, "For what that's worth."

Kerry finished his cookies and coffee and stroked the edge of the computer, admiring the compactness of it.

"She didn't put anything on it, did she? Any programs? Games?"

Doris' cockeyed smile told him she understood.

"I don't think so. She likes other people's business, but she knows a fence when she sees it and she stays on her side."

And 'Mama D' is here to make sure I know a fence when I see it and stay on my side. He felt certain Doris would do what it took to be sure he didn't take advantage of his employer's generous good nature. *All tender-hearted people should have such a shield.*

~*~

Kerry was up to his elbows in volumes, none of which was less than forty years old. He had found, with no surprise, that the volumes on the lowest shelves were the newest and were older the farther out of reach they were. They were an utter jumble of mass-production and typeset/handbound bookmaking art. As he had promised, he left them where they were unless they needed attention. In those cases, he noted the column and row in which he had found them, so he could put them back in relatively the same place if Juss wanted to keep them.

The little computer was delightfully fast, and he quickly set up a spreadsheet for the project, including a virtual map of the entire library, to be filled in as he explored the shelves. It was the best job he had ever had, even setting aside Juss and Doris' warmth and Juss' assistance to Abby.

His cell phone rang. He was delighted to see the call was from Schatzi. She seldom called him at work, so this was a rare treat.

"Hello, darling," he said.

"Oh, dear, Kerry, I'm sorry to bear bad news," Schatzi's worried voice said, "but Abby has left the building."

"I beg your pardon?"

"I've been working in my office all morning, and I came out to throw together some lunch for us and found a note: *I'm going home. I can't stay here and put you and the kids in danger. Please don't come to visit me. It isn't safe.* Kerry, the writing is shaky. You would think the KGB had a contract out on her. I should never have told her. The poor, silly girl. She apparently took a taxi — had it pick her up on the corner. I don't know what to do. I called her, and she forbade me to come bring her back or even come comfort her. What's to be done?"

"Let me think." Kerry scratched his mustache. "Ah! I'll call Mr. Delaney and have him call that female Deputy Sheriff. They want to know where Abby is all the time, at any rate, and perhaps she can reassure her or persuade her to come back to us."

Shatzi, relief evident, said, "Yes. That's exactly right. I'm sorry to bother you at work, sweetheart."

"I'm glad you did, darling. Not to worry. I'll take care of it."

He dialed Mr. Delaney's number and, Mr. Delaney being in court that day, left his message with the clerk, who promised to pass it on when the lawyer called in between court appearances.

Chapter 24

Juss came out of the Sherbourne Building and blinked in the sunlight. Her client, an executive in an optical company located on the seventh floor of the Sherbourne, had used her hour to discuss the relative merits of various weight loss programs and had all but arm-wrestled Juss in an attempt to get her, Juss, to choose. Juss had insisted that the point of having a Life Coach was to learn to make these decisions for oneself, and the client had finally plumped — Juss forgave herself the pun — on one.

Her eyes adjusted to the light and there, across Madison Street, was a narrow doorway with a sign above it reading *WJAZ Radio*.

It's a sign. Well, yes, obviously it was a sign, but it was also a *sign*. The jazz station was where Marsha Knowles' neighbor — the one she probably got along with — worked as a receptionist. Juss consulted her notebook and retrieved the name: Priscilla Bingly.

She looked both ways and trotted across the street.

I came out of the Sherbourne and saw the radio station across the street. And I thought, "I've never even considered advertising on the radio." So I decided to go over and see what their rates are. And guess who's the receptionist? You'll never guess, not in a million years. Isn't it a small, small world? Then DW would be so busy trying to get "It's a Small, Small World" out of his head, he wouldn't think about what a coincidence it was.

A woman with her hair in short silver spikes sat behind

a desk at right angles to the door, midway between the entrance and the elevators. She looked up with a formal smile. She was wearing a soft gray cashmere dress and a rope of big clunky silver beads.

"Welcome to Jazz Radio," she said. "What can we do for you today?"

"Well, uh," Juss was glad to find a name badge hiding behind the silver bobbles, "Priscilla, I'm thinking about advertising with the station."

"Oh, excellent! A lot of people do. We reach four counties, you know."

"I didn't know."

"Well, we do! Would you like me to ring our advertising manager?" She had picked up the phone and pressed a speed-dial button before Juss could answer and had hung up before Juss had decided she might as well go on and check the rates for real. "I forgot. He's out of the office today. Could I have him call you?"

"Yes, thanks." Juss gave her a business card.

"Oh, Spadena Street! That's such a cute street. We toured it once, when Harold was first thinking about relocating here — oh, thirty years ago. But real estate prices were so much lower here than in California, we decided we might as well go gated community."

"I'm thinking that would be Highgate Commons."

"Bingo!" Priscilla Bingly said, the corners of her eyes crinkling with her smile — a genuine one, this time. "Have you been there?"

"I have friends who live there. The DeSalvos."

"Oh, Paul and Genny! Such nice people."

"I *think* I've met somebody else who lives there. Margaret Cole? Something like that."

"Marsha Knowles?"

Juss snapped her fingers. "That's it! Marsha Knowles. Do you know her?"

"Why, she's my next door neighbor."

"Is she really?"

"Well, it's a small town, isn't it? Where did you meet Marsha? At the spa?"

"Could be. Could be."

"She's worked there as long as I've known her. You wouldn't think a personal trainer would make enough to live in the Commons, but apparently it pays quite well. It does at Perfect Fit, at any rate."

"I would think so." Perfect Fit was not a place many native-born Jorisburgers went. It was the kind of place where they pampered you on one hand and tortured you with their evil fitness machines on the other. "But maybe not so much. Genny tells me Marsha is still driving the wreck."

"Oh!" Priscilla flapped a dismissive hand. "She had to wait until the insurance check came in. She took the car to the shop the other day. Genny probably didn't recognize the rental car. It's a perfectly respectable brown Volvo. Not exactly Marsha's style, but nothing to object to."

"Marsha's real car is that, uh. . . ."

"Red Miata, right."

"Listen, I was visiting Genny the other day, and the gates were wide open and nobody in the guard shack. Anybody could come in. That doesn't seem safe."

"We haven't had a guard for a donkey's years. Everybody has security systems, not to mention the Neighborhood Association."

"So you'd know if somebody was, oh, poking around

somebody's car or something."

"Oh, yes. Strangers get a good once- or twice-over, believe you me."

"That's good to know."

The phone rang. Pricilla raised a finger to indicate Juss should wait and said, "Jazz Radio. What can we do for you today? One moment, please." She pushed a button and hung up. "Now." She printed a name and number on a scratchpad with the station's contact information on it, tore it off and handed it across the desk. "This is Farley Benson's direct line."

"He's the Advertising Manager?"

"He's the Advertising Manager. Give him a call and he'll set you right up."

Juss tucked the paper into her purse and left, brimming with virtue. *I came in to see about advertising and I saw about advertising.* It also set to rest the niggling worry about Marsha Knowles' safety that Kerry's theory had set vibrating.

Now, how about lunch?

~*~

Have to eat somewhere, *don't I?* Juss had been meaning to try the CT 'Scape's lunch offerings for some time. She really had.

Now she stood inside, pressed against the wall to be out of the way, and read the menu board, listening to the customers banter with the baristas and baristos, listening to what got ordered most and what the servers answered when customers asked, "What's good today?"

She got in line and ordered the special: a cup of tomato-basil soup, half a veggie club sandwich, pickle spear, home-made potato chips, and a mug of Ethiopian.

"Pick up your coffee at the end of the counter," the baristo said. "I'll bring your food to you."

"Thanks." She checked out the room and saw that the table she wanted was empty: the one by the window on the parking lot side of the building. She snagged her coffee and plunked it on the table to claim her territory.

Here's where Abby sat. She settled into the seat. *What can I see? The front part of the parking lot, the street.* Turning her head, she saw more of the parking lot, tree-lined Slot Street and the side entrance of Decker's Records. If she leaned across the table and craned her head, she could see a little more of the lot, *maybe* where Abby's car had been parked. But Abby had said she hadn't done that. Or, rather, she *hadn't* said she *had* done that, which wasn't the same thing, was it?

"Excuse me?" The good-looking counterman stood by the table, a plate in one hand and a bowl in the other. "Looking for something?"

"A friend of mine was in here a couple of days ago, and she thought somebody might have messed with her car. I wanted to see if she could see the car from where she said she was sitting."

"Mind saying who it was? If she's a regular, I might know her."

"Abigail Andrews."

He thought, then shook his head. "Don't know the name."

"She has brown fuzzy hair and hazel eyes and she's always kind of nervous—"

"Oh, *Abby!* Sure, I know Abby. She's my buddy. Somebody messed with her car? What did they do, key it?"

144

He pantomimed scraping something along a surface and made a hideous *kkkkkkkk!* sound.

"No."

"Hey! I bet I saw 'em!"

Juss whipped out her notebook. "Tell me."

He sat down. "I was sitting here, talking to Abby. A car pulled in on the other side of hers and somebody got out. Then they got back in their car and pulled out."

"What did they look like?"

He shook his head. "That, I couldn't tell you. I could tell their door opened, and I could see, like, a figure, but it was through this glass and two car windows, and one of Abby's windows is all buggered up from that wreck she was in last April — You know about that? Okay. Anyway, I couldn't see who it was. Couldn't even tell if it was a woman or a man."

"What kind of car was it?"

"Didn't really see the car. From here, all I could see was a vehicle pulling in. See, the trees and bushes are pretty much in the way. It was a black car, though, I could tell that."

"Solid black?"

"Well, mostly black, I'd say, anyway." He rapped on the table as a period to the conversation. "Gotta get back to work. Nice talking to you. Tell my buddy I said hello, okay?"

"Okay." Juss wrote, stared at what she'd written, put a comma in and stared some more.

Not very helpful, actually. Except that we know for sure that somebody was by Abby's car. She shifted uneasily. She had uncovered what might be important evidence. That might be considered messing in police business. *Well, but I didn't ask him anything. He came up and started talking to me.* She wasn't certain DW would accept that. In fact, she was pretty damned sure he'd take strong exception to her having come here in the first place. *It's a free country. I can eat where I want.*

In fact, the food was so good she determined to come more often. *So there.*

~*~

Juss pushed her lunch dishes aside and set up her laptop. The sight of so many people enjoying free high-speed access made her want to join the party, although she didn't have anything to do online. *In fact, though, come to think of it. . . .*

She opened a series of browser tabs, brought up search engines in each of them, and went to work.

"Marsha Knowles" and Jorisburg. "Abigail Andrews" and Jorisburg. Court records. Newspaper reports. Browsing happily, she hardly noticed the baristo taking her empty dishes and bringing her a refill on her coffee.

She found a notice of the court proceedings with a transcript. She could imagine Abby on the stand, could hear her voice stammering the "um"s and "uh"s, could imagine those — let's face it — slightly buggy eyes with their look of blank panic.

Jack Pitt's questions and remarks came across as sarcastic and condescending — insulting to Abby, her witnesses, and even Judge Walkin. The only person in the courtroom he treated with respect was Marsha Knowles, and he treated her as if she were a saint and a genius.

Odd, since you'd think a saint and a genius would know that if one car has a broken headlight and another car has a crunched rear door, it's not believable to insist that the

146

one with the crunched door hit the one with the broken headlight. Hel-lo-o? And in the face of two witnesses?

Pitt's argument was that Abby had been driving uninsured and, under the law, she was automatically at fault in any accident she was in. That was the law. Driving uninsured was illegal, and one of the penalties it carried was automatic guilt in an accident. In language that came across as a nose-tweak even in legalese, Pitt pointed this out to Judge Walkin, who informed him, right there in the transcript, that he didn't need anyone to give him lessons on the law.

It wasn't surprising that Judge Walkin had declared himself unable to decide the case and had dismissed it.

Let's see; what else can we find?

Marsha Knowles, Fitness Instructor, Perfect Fit Spa. Picture? Picture!

So this was the infamous Marsha Knowles. The picture showed a pert, petite woman in a skin-tight leotard or work-out suit or whatever they were called. It went from ankle to wrists to neck, but there wasn't a wrinkle in it. It showed every available attraction of a firm and bosomy body. She was smiling, red lips and white teeth in a tan face, almond eyes nearly closed, black hair pulled back or slicked down into a shining helmet.

Maybe not such a wonder that a skirt-chaser like Pitt would use a point of law to make time with such a pretty woman. But what was Marsha's angle? What had Abby said about it? Something about insurance?

Well, what else?

Marsha Knowles, graduate blah blah high school, blah blah college — scads of those all over the world. Apparently, Marsha Knowles wasn't a terribly unique name. Few names were, after all. *Not everybody is blessed with a name nobody else in the whole freaking world was likely to—*

Oh, ho! What have we here? A LiveJournal page? Do we have a LiveJournal page? Juss clicked on the link. *We have a LiveJournal page! And bless my soul, we call it Marsha Knowles Knows. Ah, ego! Gotta love it!*

The picture on the home page showed Marsha with her head down, looking up over the rims of silver-lensed sunglasses. Juss clicked to see the picture gallery. Marsha in her Spa suit. Marsha in very short shorts and a halter top — not an ounce of fat on her. *She looks like she could lift weights with her boobs.* Marsha in a slinky gold dress with a red dragon embroidered around the high neck, sitting on a couch and looking at the camera with a furtive smile, a man sitting next to her, bending over to pick up a drink from the coffee table, ponytail hanging forward over his shoulder. . . . *Could that be Jack Pitt, caught on webcam? Oh, Marsha, you sly fox!*

There were pages of long entries, some of them qualifying as rants, about the accident and its repercussions. Juss saved them all to her hard drive so she could read them at her leisure, and in case Marsha smartened up and deleted them. Juss was only scanning them, but the picture Marsha painted of herself was not an attractive one. Of course, anybody who could make Abby mad enough to get up on her hind legs and say "bitch" was pretty much guaranteed to be an unattractive person.

According to Marsha, she had been driving along, minding her own business, when Abby had pulled screeching out in front of her *and,* by some quirk of physics, apparently, had *also* run into her. *Kind of like hurting a guy's knuckles by smashing your face into his hand, I guess.* According to Marsha, Abby had been rude and abrasive, not to mention stupid. The officer who filed the report was stupid. The witnesses were stupid. The judge was stupid.

Okay, I can't read much of this at one sitting. Is there anything else? No?

She closed her laptop and snugged it into its carrying case and sat back to finish her coffee before her next appointment.

Chapter 25

Abby wished she smoked, so she could have a cigarette. She was sure it would calm her nerves, but it was too late to take up the habit now. For one thing, she'd have to leave her apartment to buy a pack, and she wasn't about to do that.

She called Mark McGuire and Jeremy Craft to mind. Both older men, both irritable about the process, both outraged at Marsha Knowles' recklessness, both very kind about Abby's misfortune. When she actually thought about the men, she couldn't believe there was any basis for Kerry and Schatzi's fear. It seemed silly. But, when she thought of the clips on the news, showing Jack Pitt's body inside that dark building, yellow police tape holding gawkers at bay, bright lights and police cars in the picture, and the reporter interviewing Carlton Cornflower, she didn't know what to believe, and it seemed safer to be afraid than to not be.

It was only 1:30. Maybe she could go to the CT 'Scape for a coffee and a sandwich for a late lunch. She felt as if she'd spent half the day here, pacing and watching the news or listening to reports on the radio or re-reading the accounts in the paper. "Police following leads", "confident of an arrest", "no comment". What did all that mean? Did it mean they were closing in on the culprit or closing in on *her?*

She should never have left Kerry and Schatzi's. *Yes, I should. I did the right thing. I don't want anything bad to happen to either of them or — worse — any of the kids. I'm not safe to be around. I'm a walking target. Oh, dear.*

Her doorbell, wired from her name plaque next to the downstairs door, rang in her apartment.

Abby jumped, then stood very still. Her toes and fingertips tingled as blood rushed to fuel the pounding of her heart. She heard her own shallow breathing. She heard a bird singing in the tree outside her front window.

The bell was a courtesy; the front door was only locked after dark. Downstairs, the front door opened. Whoever was coming up the stairs was walking quietly. Was it one person or two? A familiar footstep, or a stranger's? *How can people tell? Feet on stairs are feet on stairs — how can you recognize one set from another?*

Three raps on the door made Abby jump again. *Pretend I'm not here. Kerry or Schatzi would have called and said they were coming over.*

Three louder raps. Abby held her breath.

"Miss Andrews? Are you there?"

She'd heard that bass voice before.

"Miss Andrews? It's Alan Cunningham. The police officer from the other morning? Sheriff Cornflower asked me to check on you. Are you there?"

Giddy with relief, Abby started breathing again.

"Yes! Yes, I'm here. I'm fine. I'm all right."

She fumbled at the locks and opened the door.

The tall young officer was off duty, dressed in pale blue jeans and a tan t-shirt with the sheriff's department's logo in the upper left. He held a bike helmet in his gloved hands. Abby remembered those gloves as if *they* had opened her car door, *they* had taken pictures, *they* had called the sheriff, and not the policeman.

"I'm sorry to keep you waiting, Officer . . . Deputy . . . Mister . . . Cunningham."

"Alan, please. Call me Alan, Miss Andrews, please."

"Alan. Come in, Alan. Do come in. And call me Abby." *I'm dithering. Blithering. A blithering idiot.* "Would you like some tea? Or coffee? Or I could get you a beer . . . except that I don't have any."

Alan laughed, his helmet in his hands.

Should I offer to take it? Or would that be like offering to take his gun or his badge?

"Won't you sit down? Won't you have some tea? Or coffee? Or. . . ."

"Or beer you don't have? Heh."

She felt herself blushing.

Alan stepped into the apartment so she could close the door. "Mind if I put my helmet down?"

"No, I wish you would. I mean — Oh, I don't know what I mean. Would you like some tea?"

"Tea is fine. Iced tea? Sweet tea?"

"Well, no. But I can make it and then put some sugar and ice in it."

"That sounds fine. Thanks."

"The kitchen is in here, in the . . . in the kitchen." *Oh! I am such an idiot!*

Abby managed to make it to the kitchen and managed to remember where the saucepan was. She turned on the water full blast and, before she could turn it off, the burst of water hit the bottom of the pan and bounced back up like a fountain, soaking the window, the counter, and her head.

Alan came running in answer to her yelp. She saw him through strands of dripping hair — saw him stop in the doorway, take in what had happened, and laugh. Not just laugh. He turned red in the face, leaned against the doorpost, held his sides, and slid down to sit on the floor.

Abby put the pan down in the sink, got a dishtowel, and dried herself as best she could. Alan was still laughing. She mopped up the water on the counter, window, and floor as he wiped his eyes, struggled to his feet, and gasped,

"I'm sorry. I'm so sorry."

"It's all right." She was calm now. Her nervousness was gone. Everything was normal. Nothing was special. Nothing to get excited about. She was one of those sad-sack clowns who do stupid things and make other people roar with laughter. How very nice for other people. She filled the pan and put it on the stove — even turned on the correct burner — and set up the makings of a pitcher of iced tea.

"No, I'm really sorry. That was so rude. I couldn't help it. You're so. . . ."

"So funny. I understand. People laugh at me a lot. I'm used to it."

"No, no!" Alan came closer to her. He leaned against the sink, straightened up, and stared at the wet blotch the sink had left on his jeans. "You missed a spot," he said, and a strangled *har* escaped before he could hold it back.

"I'm a clown," Abby said, calm inside and out. "I know."

"You're not a clown!" Alan scowled savagely. "Who says you're a clown?"

Startled, Abby said, "I do things like—" she waved at the damp counter, "—this. I can't write a check at the grocery store if there's anybody behind me in line without screwing it up. If people aren't laughing at me, it's because they're goggling at me because they can't believe I'm such a goof-ball. Now Kerry and Schatzi and the kids could have been in danger because I coned out and didn't mail my car insurance check. I'm not even funny. I'm pathetic."

Still scowling, he said, "You're *adorable*."

Abby blinked. *What did he say?* "Excuse me?"

"I said you're adorable." Now Alan was scowling and blushing.

Maybe he has that thing where people use the wrong word when they get excited, and the laughing triggered it. He probably means, "You're stupid." Great — now I've damaged a policeman.

The scowl vanished, and the blush faded to red spots on each cheek. He looked like a Jolly Copper doll, if there were such a thing.

"I oughtn't to be saying this, you know. Maybe it's okay, since I'm, you know, off-duty and that, but I probably still oughtn't to be saying it, you being officially not off the suspect list yet and all, but. . . ."

His gaze roamed over her face. "I've been on this beat for two years, you know. I remember the first time I saw you come out of the apartment carrying that backpack with, you know, the kitten on it. I almost fell off my bicycle, staring at you, you looked so precious."

Well, this is . . . alarming. There had to be something wrong with a man who looked at her and saw *anything*, let alone something precious!

"I thought about introducing myself sometime, you know, riding up and saying, what they taught us, like, 'Hi, I'm Alan Cunningham. I'm the neighborhood face of Jorisburg's Cop on the Beat program. If you ever need assistance, or just want to pass the time of day for a couple of minutes, I'm your man.' I did put a flyer in your mailbox. You know, in case you didn't get one when they started the program."

"Oh, yes," Abby said weakly. She vaguely remembered the flyer in her mailbox, though she didn't remember an earlier one. She remembered worrying that the neighborhood might not be safe, if they had to have a special cop on the beat. She thought she had folded the flyer and stuck it in a drawer somewhere.

"But I never stopped and introduced myself." Alan hung his head. "I was too shy, you know? You were too sweet. You were too precious."

Speechless.

"And then, you know, that woman ran into you." His scowl was back, worse than ever. "When I thought about losing you — you know, losing any chance of ever talking to you, maybe getting to know you better. . . ." He shook his head. "The water's boiling."

"Excuse me? — Oh!" Her mind a confusion of unaccustomed input, her body worked automatically until she had set the timer for the tea to steep. She stood then, staring at the timer as it counted down the seconds, afraid to look at Alan again.

"I can't believe I was lucky enough to be there when you found, you know, the thing that made you ask for help. I can't believe I got to ride to your rescue. And then what did I do?" She jumped as he smacked himself upside the head. "I went into cop mode and got all Sergeant Joe Friday with you."

"You had to do your job," Abby said. "But you were very kind."

"You thought so? I wasn't all, you know, cold and official? I didn't put you off?"

She turned around to face him.

"No. You were perfect."

"You were so scared and all. I wanted to hug you and say, 'There, there. I'll take care of you.' But all I could do was tell you to call somebody else! I knew it would be your boyfriend."

"I don't have a boyfriend. I called my cousin."

Joy turned his awkward face beautiful. "You don't have a boyfriend? Really?"

She almost said *Who would want to date a dope like me?* but she was beginning to hope.

"Really."

The timer went off.

~*~

Abby and Alan sat on the opposite ends of the couch, sipping tea and talking. The only thing they had in common was a love of baseball, but that was enough to keep the conversation going — that, and the fact that neither of them wanted the conversation to end.

This was one of those times Abby lived for: when she could lose herself in the moment, when she could forget her self-consciousness and float on the experience, when her inner critic went to sleep and let her enjoy her own company.

The phone rang.

"Hello?"

A friendly, nasal voice on the other end said, "Hi, Abby? Abigail Andrews?"

"Yes, it is."

"Oh, good! I've been trying to get hold of you. Listen,

this is Marsha Knowles. You ran into my car?"

A shot of sheer fury ran through her.

The voice went on. "Anyway, I'm suing you for the damages to my car. So expect to get some papers in the mail. I hope you still have that lawyer."

"How can you—? What are you—?"

Marsha laughed, as if they were sharing a joke.

"I'll tell you what — If you want to come by the Spa — you know, the Perfect Fit? Do you know where it is?" When Abby didn't answer, she said, louder, "Do. You. Know. Where. It. Is?"

"Yes," Abby choked out.

"Well, come by around three and we'll talk about a settlement. Can you make it?"

No. I don't want to leave the apartment. But. . . .

"Well, can you or can't you? Never mind. I'll be in the food court at three. That's when I have my break. If you can make it, fine. If you can't, too bad. Bye."

Abby dropped the phone to the floor instead of putting it on the coffee table, she was shaking so with rage.

"What is it?" Alan asked, retrieving her phone.

"It's that bitch — excuse me, that woman who ran into me. She's suing me for damages."

"*She* hit *you!* Any fool could see that somebody hit *you*, not the other way around. Can she do that?"

"She can try. She can keep my life in a mess and drag those poor men who testified for me back into court — if they'll come."

"They could have been subpoenaed for the criminal trial, but maybe not, you know, for a civil court claim. I don't know about that. You got a lawyer?"

"Mr. Byrum? I could call him." A wave of relief washed

her ashore. "I do. I do have a lawyer. DW Delaney." She reached for her purse, then remembered. "I gave his card to my cousin Kerry."

"Can I use your phone to look him up for you?"

She nodded. His thumbs flew over the tiny keyboard.

"Got it," he said. "Now." He pushed two buttons at once and Abby heard a tell-tale click.

"Oh, I do that all the time. I have so many pictures of my screen that I took by accident."

"Well, now you have one I took on purpose. If you lose track of this site with Mr. Delaney's number on it, you can find the picture of it in your photos."

He handed her her phone, his hand lingering in her palm as she received the device.

After a long moment, he said, "I got to go. Mom's expecting me for lunch, and I'm late already."

"Oh, I'm so sorry!"

"No, no! Part of my job and all. And besides. . . ." Those precious red spots came back to his cheeks.

Abby luxuriated in a warm fuzzy feeling. It was almost like when you have a headache and take some pain reliever and there's one brief moment when your head still throbs but the pain reliever is working and you can't actually feel the pain any more. Marsha was going to sue her, but she wasn't afraid or powerless. She had a lawyer, she had family, she had a firm — if odd — friend in Juss, and a handsome young man had looked up a number for her, not because he thought she couldn't do it, but because he wanted to.

Chapter 26

As Juss gathered her purse, jacket, keys, and laptop to leave, the handsome baristo came to bus her table.

He touched her lightly on the hand and said, "You're a friend of Abby's, right?"

"Yes, I am."

"Do you think what I told you might be important? About seeing somebody near her car?"

"It could be." She took out her notebook and pen. "Could I get your name and a phone number, if you'd be willing to tell about it? I don't mean in court."

"Oh, I got no sweat about telling it in court. Sure. I'm Benjamen Joosten, but if you ask for me around here, everybody calls me Beej." He gave his number. "But you think I'd better tell it to her lawyer? He's right over there."

Trying to look innocent with a guilty conscience, Juss smiled toward where he nodded, but DW was nowhere in sight. Then she realized he must have meant the lawyer who had represented Abby in the court case. Robert Byrum, that was it.

"She has a different lawyer now," she said, guilt receding at the speed of light, "but I'd like a word with this one, anyway. Which guy is he?"

"Tall dude, blond hair, black turtleneck, and black-and-gray tweed coat."

His hair was beyond blond, almost a baby-white. It was so pale, fine, and thin that it was only visible because his wet-look gel darkened it and gathered its wisps into spikes.

"Got him. Thanks. I think Abby might need you to talk to the new lawyer."

"Whatever. I mean that. And tell my little buddy that Beej said hello."

"I'll do that."

Juss maneuvered to the lawyer's table.

"Hi," she said. "Robert Byrum?"

He stood up. Then he stood up some more. *He must be six-four, six-five. Taller than DW, but thin.* He smiled and held out a hand.

"That's me. And you are?"

"Juss Chocolate. I'm a friend of Abigail Andrews."

"Abigail Andrews." He looked blank, then retrieved the memory. "Oh, yes. Driving uninsured."

"Are you allowed to talk about that?"

"The case is over and settled, so, yes, in general. How do you know Abby?"

"I met her through her cousin Kerry."

"Won't you sit down?" He gestured to the chair across the table from his, closed his laptop and, after Juss was seated, sat back down. "Would you like something? Chai? Latté?"

"Nothing for me, thanks, but you go ahead."

"No, I've been here all morning; I'm floating. Abigail Andrews. I met her through her cousin Kerry, too, in a way. They were in the lobby of the Justice Center, wandering around like a couple of lost lambs. I was waiting for a case to come up and improving the shining hours by passing out my card to anybody who looked like they needed representation and didn't have any." He tilted his chair back onto two legs. "I'm not a storefront lawyer, I'm a coffee house lawyer. No office, no secretary, no overhead. I work cheap. A lot of people need cheap, but nobody needs no good. I'm cheap, but I'm good."

"Apparently. You steered Abby through a nightmare, she tells me."

"Yeah." He pulled at his earlobe. "That was a weird one. I've handled at least a dozen driving uninsured cases since I started. They're all the same. Client goes into night court, pleads guilty, pays a fine, promises to get insurance. Client shows up again with proof of insurance, gets sentenced to car school, possibly a few hours of community service, does it, gets paper in the mail saying it's all over and keep your nose clean." He clunked all four chair legs onto the floor and tapped a quick drumbeat on the tabletop. "This one didn't go that way, and I don't know why. All the Prosecutors in this county do it that way. Jack Pitt always does it that way. This time, not."

"No idea why?"

He shook his head. "Not unless he *wanted* to tick off Judge Walkin. And that's possible."

"They didn't get along? I didn't know that."

"I don't know if it was anything personal, but Jack Pitt was pretty strong behind Peterson for judge in the race against Walkin. Common knowledge."

Juss was embarrassed to admit she never knew anything about the judges. She never missed a chance to vote, but she never followed the judicial races and always left those boxes unchecked. She resolved that it wouldn't happen again.

Byrum said, "Pitt and Peterson are two of a kind. Good-ol'-boy petticoat-pushers, you know what I mean?"

"They like the ladies?"

"Like 'em more if they aren't ladies." Byrum wiggled his nearly-nonexistent eyebrows.

"Speaking of Marsha Knowles," Juss said.

Byrum nearly choked. "Uh-huh, yeah," he said, wiping his eyes.

"Think there was a little hanky-panky going on there? Could that have explained Pitt pressing the case?"

"I guess it's possible." Byrum gave it consideration, but shook his head. "He's had female complainants before — ones he could have brought forward, I mean, but he didn't. If you ask me, there wasn't anything special about Marsha Knowles. Of course, there's no accounting for tastes. And if Jack Pitt had any taste, he wouldn't look beyond his own wife. Barbara Pitt — now there is a lady."

"You know her?"

It always bemused Juss, how gossipy men were. Women were supposed to be the gossips, but she had found men equally eager to dish the dirt.

Byrum answered, as if they'd known each other all their lives, "She's a friend of my wife's. Nice lady. She deserves better than that run-around hound." He looked up quickly and blinked. "Why am I telling you all this stuff?"

Juss smiled and shrugged. She thought, *Because I pumped you*, but she said, "People do. I only stopped by to say hi, and to make sure it's ethical if another lawyer represents Abby on something that might or might not be related."

"Ethical? Oh, sure — any client can have any lawyer she or he chooses. Nothing to do with ethics. Who's the lawyer, if you don't mind my asking?"

"DW Delaney. He's my lawyer."

162

"Oh, sure, everybody knows Delaney. He's good. He's very good. But — none of my business — can she afford him?"

"It's cool. It's covered."

"Okay. Okay, then. Tell her I wish her well with whatever it is. She's a nice lady."

Juss checked her watch. "Whoa — I'd better get going. I have to be in New Brighton in fifteen minutes."

"Plenty of time, plenty of time," Byrum said, but he stood up to say goodbye.

Juss stood and shook hands with him, waved to Beej, and hustled out.

I happened to run into him, DW. I was minding my own business (I was, too!) and there he was.

And there was bad blood between Jack Pitt and Judge Walkin, and friends of Barbara Pitt — including Robert Byrum — hated Jack Pitt for the way he treated her. It's no wonder the guy ended up dead. They probably rented a bus so they could all *get a piece of his hide.*

She wondered if Pitt had a blog. *Now that might be a thing to know.* She wished she had thought to look for that while she was connected. *Maybe later.* She thought about the kind of things Pitt might write about. *Maybe not.*

Chapter 27

After Alan left, Abby sat down with the phone in her hand and stared at Mr. Delaney's contact page on her phone's screen. She was proud that she hadn't called Kerry or Schatzi. Poor people — they had been so patient with her. *And I even dragged Kerry's boss into it.* She blushed, painfully this time. *She must think Kerry comes from a crazy family. It might cost him his job. And, speaking of cost, what is a lawyer like Mr. Delaney costing Kerry? He says it's nothing, but that can't be true. They're keeping that from me, so I won't worry. Poor little Abby, can't handle reality.* Well, how far off was that? Had she done such a great job of handling reality? Not so much.

Okay. First thing, don't run up any more bills with Mr. Delaney. *Call Mr. Byrum — I know I can afford him.*

She dug through piles of scrap paper stuffed into the end table drawers until she unearthed Mr. Byrum's business card. The number on it was for his cell phone, so it should reach him wherever he was. Or not. She got his voicemail, froze, and hung up. Okay, what should she say? She took a scrap of paper and a pen and wrote it out: *Mr. Byrum, this is Abigail Andrews.* No need to leave a phone number when Caller ID would tell him that. *You defended me in a driving uninsured case in April when Jack Pitt took it to criminal court. Marsha Knowles, the woman who claimed I hit her, just called and said she's suing me for damages. I'm going to meet her at three to talk about it. If we can't settle it and have to go to court, can you be my lawyer?*

164

Was that too long? She didn't think it was, if she didn't start stammering. She read it to herself a couple of times, called Mr. Byrum's number, and said her piece. So, that was that.

She took the phone book onto her lap and turned from Attorneys to Car Rental. The Clunker Brothers specialized in cars that were on their last legs. Their rentals weren't pretty — often, they weren't particularly comfortable — but they were cheap, and the rental lot was only about six blocks away. A walk would do her good. Maybe she wouldn't be so mad when she got to the Spa. And after she left Marsha, she could go across the road to Blankenbaker Mall and shop for Joel's birthday.

Chapter 28

Juss was glad to see Kerry's green VW in front of her house. She wished Schatzi would be there, too, but she knew she wouldn't.

The kitchen was empty, so she went on through to the office. Also empty. She put her laptop on her desk, hung her jacket and purse in the office closet, and checked the answering machine for messages. *Nothing.*

For once, she was glad. *Why?* She was usually as happy as a pig in mud when she had lots of calls from clients, lots of problems to solve, hands to hold, noses to wipe. What the problems were never made any difference. Suddenly, she was getting picky?

"That you, Baby Girl?" Doris' voice came from the living room.

"No," Juss said, according to their tradition, the origin of which was lost in the mists of time, "it's a burglar, coming through the door in broad daylight."

A surprised *haw!* from the living room told her where Kerry was.

When she was in the office doorway, Doris came out and told her, "I thawed and heated some of that banana bread you made. You want to see if you can talk Kerry into taking a break? 'Cause I can't."

"Sure."

"He is a worker."

A hot shaft of resentment shot through her as she stood in the doorway, not going to fetch Kerry. "I'm a worker, too."

Doris stopped between one stride and another and turned wide eyes on Juss. "I know you are."

"I had two appointments today. I know that doesn't sound like much, but they were long appointments. I do things for people. Maybe not for many people, but the people I help really appreciate it."

Obviously baffled, Doris said, "I know. What in the world brought this on?" When Juss didn't say anything — couldn't sort out what to say — Doris said, "The banana bread's getting cold, sugar. Come on and let's have it while it's warm. Mama D missed having you around today. I want to sit down at the table with you and share something nice."

Juss went to the living room, more than a little baffled, herself. *What* was *that all about? I do not know.*

Juss found Kerry up a ladder, sliding a tiny red-bound volume in between two large brown ones. He was wearing one of Doris' aprons — a sort of canvas pinafore with a howling wolf stenciled on the front and *FEED ME* and *American Wolf Council* underneath — a "gift" the Council sent with a letter soliciting contributions. The apron pockets were sagging, and she realized he was wearing it to carry books up and down the ladder.

"Doris says come to the kitchen and have some banana bread. I hereby order you to take a break."

"As soon as I replace these books. I've been smelling the bread and drooling. Luckily, my clothes are protected." He patted the wolf.

"Was that your idea, or Doris'? The apron?"

He touched one of the straps. "We prefer to call it a 'load bearing safety device'," he said solemnly. "It was

Doris' idea." He reached into the right-hand pocket and pulled out another small red book and slid it into place. "I'm astounded," he said. "These books are hardly dusty at all. Surely you don't read all of them that often."

"We call in a cleaning service to dust them all once a month, and Doris dusts the ones in reach once a week."

"Ah. Excellent. More books are lost to dust and inattention than to silverfish and mice."

"Ewww!"

"Yes," he said, coming down the ladder. "It takes nerves of steel to be a librarian."

The piles of books to be repaired or discarded had grown. The discard pile was surrounded by crumbs and chunks of pages and binding.

Juss laid a hand on the pile, wishing she could heal them with a touch.

"These were very poorly made," Kerry said, "and probably saw hard use before they were shelved. None of them are inscribed — I'm noting inscriptions." He tapped a stenographer's notebook with small, precise handwriting. "If there's anything of too much sentimental value to discard, I suggest vacuum sealing it and keeping it as a solid artifact. Further use would only cause these to deteriorate more."

"Okay."

"If you want to replace the titles, you or I can look for replacements in better shape online — or, of course, reissues or higher-quality editions."

Juss wiped her hand on her pants. "They're only things," she said.

Chapter 29

Abby walked into the Perfect Fit complex conscious of her lack of muscle tone, her excess body mass index, even of the cheese, bacon, and sour cream on the loaded baked potato she'd had for a late lunch. It was reassuring to see that not everybody in the lobby, halls, and food court of the spa looked like Marsha. *Stands to reason, people come here to get fit as well as to stay fit. Duh, Abby!*

She scanned the food court for Marsha Knowles' shining black helmet of hair. Not seeing it, she went to the food counter and got a small plate of raw vegetables with honey mustard sauce and a large unsweetened hot mint tea. Comfort food for rabbits.

"Have you seen Marsha Knowles?" she asked the counterman. "I mean in the last hour or so?" *Maybe I misunderstood the time. Maybe I'm late. Maybe I'm early.*

"No," the man said. He rang up her order and counted the change into her hand. "You a friend of hers?"

"Hardly." *Oops! Too honest! Way too honest!* "I mean, not really."

He winked at her as he put an extra packet of honey on her tray. "Good luck finding her," he said. "Or not, as the case may be."

~*~

Abby polished off the last carrot stick and drained her mint tea, relishing the extra-sweet dregs where the honey

169

had settled. Still no Marsha. *She stood me up, the bitch! I might have known it was a practical joke. She's probably not really going to sue. Well,* that *part might be true.*

She checked her watch. Four o'clock. She was sure Marsha had said three. *Damn her! Damn the bitch!* Just in case, she went back to the counter after she had bussed her table.

"You didn't see Marsha come in while I was waiting, did you? I didn't miss her?"

"I didn't see her," he said. "Was she expecting you?"

"She asked me to meet her here."

"Then you didn't miss her. If Marsha wants to see you, you get seen — period, paragraph."

Abby checked her watch again. "If she comes in looking for me and if she should ask, I was here for an hour."

"Right. I'm a witness."

Abby winced but smiled at him and turned her mind to the pleasant task of buying a present for her favorite nephew.

~*~

Abby had a moment of panic in the parking lot before she remembered that the reason she couldn't find her car was that she was driving a rental. It was a little blue Datsun with more dents and dings in it than her real car. *There it is!*

She stowed her packages in the trunk. Before she got into the driver's seat, she opened the back door and inspected the seat and floor. She locked herself in behind the wheel and checked the glove compartment. Nothing weird anywhere.

She checked again when she came out of the mall after some retail therapy, buying Joel the hoodie he had showed her on his tablet and an expansion pack for Exploding Kittens.

On the way home, she remembered why she had come out in the first place; in the fun of shopping for Joel, she had forgotten about Marsha's call. Her first instinct was to be angry, but the death of Jack Pitt put a different spin on things. What if something had happened to Marsha Knowles? Besides that being a bad thing for Marsha, would she, Abby, be blamed for it?

The last of her good mood evaporated when she pulled into her parking space next to the apartment house and saw something through the viewing window in her mailbox. She had checked her mail earlier; anything in there hadn't been delivered officially.

She ignored the mailbox while she carried Joel's presents upstairs and made some tea. *Should I call Alan? Should I call Kerry? Mr. Byrum?* The one thing she was sure she should not do was touch that paper herself.

Chapter 30

The doorbell rang at 1 Spadena Street as Juss and Kerry settled in the kitchen.

Juss hadn't even scooted her chair in to the table, so she popped back up. "I'll get it."

An expressionless DW Delaney loomed on the stoop.

"Come in," she said. "What's wrong?" She had a sinking feeling that she was in trouble with her friend. *How bad was I today? How bad does he* know *I was? I didn't* mean *to be bad.*

He hung his hat and coat on the coatrack. "Is Mr. Dashingly here?"

"Yes. We're in the kitchen with Doris. Come on in." Whatever he had to say, he obviously wanted to say it once and say it to Kerry as well as to her, so she didn't ask him again what was wrong.

"Well!" Doris said, "look who the cat dragged in!" She set another place and filled another plate with banana bread while DW sat quietly, looking back and forth between Kerry and Juss. Juss fidgeted under his regard, but Kerry met his eyes with apparent equanimity. Doris poured coffee and sat. "Okay, Double-Wide, what's got your shorts all knotted up?"

DW couldn't hold back a smile and shook his head in defeat. "I'd appreciate knowing what's going on," he said. He sipped coffee, blew across the surface and sipped again. "I got a call from Robert Byrum saying he got a call from Abigail Andrews asking him to represent her in a suit for damages petitioned by Marsha Knowles."

"What?" Kerry was outraged. "That insufferable. . . ." As if at a loss for words suitable for mixed company, he clamped his lips against the rest of the sentence.

"Yes, and then he said he wanted to run it by me because Juss Chocolate had told him that *I* was Miss Andrews' lawyer."

"I happened to run into him," Juss said weakly.

"Do you know him?"

"I do now."

"Mm-hmmm."

Might as well be hung for a sheep as a goat. "Okay, I *have* been poking around, but only on the fringe!" She twiddled her fingers, demonstrating the extreme fringiness of her investigation. "I haven't seen, spoken to, written, emailed, or in any way contacted Jack Pitt's widow or daughter or any of their relatives, or Judge or Mrs. Walkin or any of their relatives."

"Or their friends?"

She gasped to signify her exasperation. "Oh, come on, DW! This is Jorisburg! Everybody knows everybody, or knows somebody who knows somebody! You can't spit on the sidewalk in front of a stranger without it getting home before you do."

"Fair enough. So tell me all about it."

Juss fetched her notebook from the office, talking the whole time. "I thought it wouldn't hurt if I asked a few questions, sort of in general, to get the big picture, you know, about the whole court case thing and the whole accident thing — Ooo! I didn't even think about talking to the cop who wrote the ticket at the accident!"

DW raised a cautionary finger. "Continue to not even think about it."

"Oo-kaay." She plopped into her chair, her notebook's spiral binding clattering on the table. Doris stroked her hair and got refills on the coffee while Juss turned to the book's first page.

"Did you cook this up after you got back from Abby's day before yesterday," DW asked, "or even before you left? Oh — never mind — I remember now." He pantomimed writing on the table: "*List of suspects.*"

"And I haven't spoken to any of them," Juss said virtuously.

"And while I was taking Abby to make her statement in the courthouse, you and Kerry stood in place and talked quietly amongst yourselves?"

"Well. . . . Before anybody got there, I went up to Judge Walkin's office—" she raised her voice to over-ride DW's protest, "—and talked to his clerk! Not to him, to his clerk. It was kind of gossipy girl-talk. She volunteered it. Mostly. She said that Judge Walkin and his wife were angry and nervous about Pitt dragging the case out, and she said that Pitt was a big flirt, to the point of sexual harassment."

"Everybody who worked in the justice system knew that. He's always been like that. Got his face smacked for him more than once in high school. Got his nose bloodied by a girl's boyfriend once, got shoved around by a vigilante group of boys who claimed they were defending the honor of the women of Roosevelt High, got his eye blacked. His proclivities were not unknown."

"So maybe somebody wasn't going to take it anymore."

"Good work, Sherlock! The police would never have thought of that."

Juss quietly closed her notebook and drank her coffee, looking at a corner of the room where nobody was.

It was silent around the table. Then DW said, "I'm sorry." When she didn't respond, he said, "I'm sorry, Juss. Mrs. Tiggy-Winkle?"

She had to laugh at that. *He knew I would, the stinker!* He had started calling her that in her teen years, when she had spiked her hair and had thought she looked very dark and threatening, and he had said she looked like a hedgehog washerwoman from a kid's book.

"Tell me the rest of it," he said. "I'll be good."

"Well, she told me all that. And then I already told you I ran into Officer Cunningham, and he said he was sure Abby didn't know what was in her car."

"Yes, and *then* I took Abby to make her statement. What happened *then?*"

Juss opened her book and stared at her notes. "Uh, then I went upstairs to the Prosecutor's office and copied down the names on the plaque outside the door. I didn't go in."

"And then?"

"Then I came back down."

"And?"

"And nothing. Kerry and I sat down and I showed him what I'd found out."

Kerry cleared his throat. "You needn't protect me. I told Mr. Delaney that I slipped into the Personnel Office and got the names of the employees in the Prosecutor's Office."

"First," DW said, "let me say that you two deserve each other."

Juss beamed at Kerry, who grinned back at her.

"This is not a game," DW said. "A man is dead. If what was in Miss Andrews' car is what I think it is, that death was deliberate and, at the very least, somebody has so little regard for Miss Andrews they want her implicated. What Mr. Dashingly found out is that Miss Andrews' two witnesses were angry about lost work time and the loss of money that work loss represented."

"I knew it!" Juss said. She waved her hand triple-time, as if erasing a chalkboard. "DW, I know this isn't a game. I take it seriously, even if I do get a kick out of finding out things." She suddenly felt very sober. A sorrow settled on her spirit. "I don't think it's 'fun' that a man is dead, not even a man as unpleasant as everybody thought Jack Pitt was. I'm excited about helping Abby. Poking around in things is what I do, and I like it that it could help keep Abby safe. I wanted to poke around where the police might not bother to look, or might not look until after people forgot how people felt or how they acted or what they said. But I might have stepped into something I didn't mean to today."

"Robert Byrum?"

"Well, something else first."

DW looked at Doris and said, "More."

Doris hooked a thumb at the coffeemaker and said, "You know where it is, Counselor."

"I mean, she has more to confess!"

Juss turned a page. "I was right across the street, so I went to WJAZ and talked to the receptionist, who is Marsha Knowles' next door neighbor."

"And you know this how?"

"Uh, I went out to Great-grandmama's old house yesterday and visited with Genny DeSalvo."

DW was surprised into immobility. "You went to the Commons? Doris went with you, though."

"I went alone."

"Were you okay?"

"I was fine. But Genny told me Marsha's neighbor was the only person who could stand her. So I did *happen* to have an appointment across the street from where the neighbor — Priscilla Bingly — works, and I popped in and *I really did* think I might buy some commercial time on the radio, so it was actually legitimate, too."

"Anything else?"

"Marsha has her car in the shop. Seems like she would want it still damaged, if she's going to sue Abby, but I guess she has the estimate and she'll have the bill. But the Commonsers were getting all bent out of shape over her driving a wrecked car on their pretty street, so I guess she felt like she'd pushed her luck as far as she could."

"I wonder who her lawyer is."

"Maybe I could find out." When DW shot her an exasperated look, she grinned and said, "Gotcha!"

He got himself another cup of coffee, waving it in mock threat at Juss.

"No more for me, thanks," she said.

He served Doris and Kerry, cut himself another piece of banana bread, and said, "What else?"

"Well. . . . Then I was hungry, so I went to that coffee house Abby likes. The CT 'Scape. And that's where I met Robert Byrum, who *just happened* to be there. But first, the guy who pointed Robert Byrum out to me, a friend of Abby's, Benjamen Joosten, sat down at the same table with

177

me, the table where Abby said she sat the morning Jack Pitt was killed. And he said, Beej did, Benjamen Joosten did, that he was sitting in that same chair that morning when Abby was in, and he saw somebody pull up next to her car and then leave without coming in for coffee."

She read to them from her notes, then told them about Robert Byrum's connection to Pitt and his wife.

"And I was worried about getting into stuff that might be important to the police investigation," she said piously. "So I was going to call you as soon as I got through with my afternoon appointment and got home and unwound a little."

"So," DW asked Kerry, "do you know anything about this suit for damages?"

"This is the first I've heard of it."

"Do you happen to know where your cousin is?"

"She said she was going back to her apartment."

"So you don't know where she is?"

"If she isn't at home, I don't. Do you?"

Juss' cell phone rang. She checked the Caller ID. *Unknown.* She almost pushed *Ignore,* but she read the number out loud.

"That's Abby's!" Kerry said.

Naturally, she answered.

"Juss, this is Abby," the breathless voice said. "I'm sorry to bother you. I didn't know who to call. I've made such a mess of things. I don't know what to do."

She called me. She called me. Juss felt as if she'd quieted a baby who cried at everybody else.

"What's wrong, Abby?"

"I don't know. I mean I'm not sure. Maybe nothing. It's probably a flyer about no parking on the even side of the street on Wednesday or something. But I don't know."

"There's something — what? — slipped under your door or in your mailbox?"

"In my mailbox. I haven't touched it."

"Good girl. Hang on a minute." She repeated what Abby had said.

"Ask her who her attorney is," DW said.

"DW says Robert Byrum called him and said you wanted him to represent you. He wants to know if he's fired or what."

With a catch in her voice, Abby said, "Marsha Knowles called and said she's going to sue me for damages to her car. I have to have a lawyer for that, and I can't afford Mr. Delaney."

"Yes, you can."

"No, I can't! I can't let Kerry and Schatzi foot the bill, and I can't let you do it for me. I'm not a charity case."

Whoa! Hurting my ear! She held the phone away from her head and raised astonished eyebrows at the others around the table.

"I never intended it as a charity case," Juss said sternly, and pulled a *What do I say next?* face at Doris.

Doris pantomimed dusting and typing.

Juss said, "I was going to say that I understand you're between jobs at the moment. Kerry can tell you that I called him in as a secretary, but I found out about his library degree and I have him cataloging the library my grandmother left me. That means I still need a secretary. Can you type?"

"Um. Yes."

"It doesn't have to be fast, as long as you can catch any mistakes either of us makes."

"I can do that."

"Would you object to giving us a hand with the housecleaning? My business is keeping me from doing all I should and Doris isn't as young as she used to be. — Ow!" She covered the phone and whispered, "Pinching isn't nice."

Abby said, "No, I wouldn't mind. I like housework. It's very soothing."

"Soothing. Yeah. That's how I feel about it. And you could help Kerry with the books, too, maybe. Well, then, you could work for me and then your legal needs would be covered as a fringe benefit, like Doris' and Kerry's are."

She held her breath, wondering if Abby would buy it, and gave a thumbs up when Abby said, "I guess that makes sense. I mean, thank you."

"So is DW your lawyer, or is Robert Byrum your lawyer?"

"Um. . . . Mr. Delaney? I guess?"

"Mr. Delaney, it is."

"Tell her I'll be right over," DW said.

"We'll be right over," Juss said. "Sit tight."

~*~

"It's a free country," Juss protested, jangling her keys in a way she knew got on Delaney's nerves. "I'm the one she called. And this might not be anything to do with the case. It might be an ad for a pizza special. Then won't you feel silly?"

"No."

"You said Kerry could come."

"Kerry is her closest relative."

"Actually," Kerry said, "her mother is living, but she has a condominium in Arizona."

Juss said, "You said Kerry could come, and he isn't even her closest relative. Besides, she and I need to talk about her job. When she should start, benefits and stuff."

Doris, in the hall doorway, said, "Stop squabbling and everybody go. Bring that poor girl back here for supper. I'll have some stew and a fruit salad; that'll keep, if it takes you a while to get back. Go on — Sooner you go, sooner we can eat."

DW lifted his hat to her and said, "I thank you, but Eloise will be expecting me."

Kerry managed to look like he was bowing, although he didn't move. "I always try to eat with Schatzi and the kids and her parents. But I hope there'll be some left over for lunch tomorrow?"

"I'll put some back for you, special."

"I'll be back," Juss said, heading for the garage as the men left by the front.

"Hurry on," Doris said. "You might miss something."

Not this *kid!* Juss followed the other cars through the streets and lights to the shady peace of Abby's street.

Uh-oh. Carlton Cornflower and the forensics guys were back, on the porch, this time.

". . . upstairs calming her down," Sheriff Cornflower was telling DW and Kerry when Juss came up.

DW told Juss, "Jean Louise Young — you know, *the policewoman* — is upstairs calming Abby down."

"Awww — " the sheriff said, disgusted at the implication.

"From what?" Juss asked.

"Let's go on up," the sheriff said to DW.

"I'm her cousin," Kerry said.

"I'm her employer," Juss said. "I'm the one she called first."

Sheriff Cornflower opened his mouth, but only let out a sigh. He nodded and went in, holding the door for the others.

Chapter 31

Kerry was shocked at his cousin's appearance. Her clothes weren't tugged out of alignment, her sweater was unbuttoned over an unstained pull-over blouse instead of being mis-buttoned to the neck. Her hair was no frizzier than usual and she was sitting, drinking (probably) tea. She rose and put down her cup when they came in. Put it securely on the end table, without dropping the cup or spilling the liquid.

Mr. Delaney took off his hat and coat, saying, "Tell me you didn't say anything."

"I asked if she'd like coffee or a cup of tea. And then I asked if she wanted milk and sugar or lemon."

"We were waiting for you, Wide Man," Deputy Young said, apparently meaning Mr. Delaney.

"Tea, anyone?" Abby asked.

"Me," Juss said. "Earl Grey. Hot. Cream and sugar."

"Never mind," Mr. Delaney said. "Has anyone told my client what the police presence here is all about? Did she call you?"

The sheriff said, "No, she didn't, as a matter of fact. And, when we knocked on her door and asked if we could look in her mailbox, she said we'd have to wait for you. She seemed upset." He looked at the deputy, who shrugged.

"I *was* upset," Abby said to Mr. Delaney. "But I knew you were coming, so I got over it." Her mouth snapped shut, telling Kerry that she had been about to say something else, but had remembered Mr. Delaney's caution.

183

Mr. Delaney spoke to the sheriff. "If she didn't call you, what brings you to her mailbox?"

The sheriff answered with his own question. "Is it all right with you if we check out the mailbox?"

Mr. Delaney asked Abby, "I'd like to speak to you privately."

"Come in the kitchen."

Delaney put a hand on Juss' shoulder. "Stay!"

Kerry watched Juss try to control herself as she eyed the sheriff. She lost the struggle.

"Do you carry handcuffs?" she asked.

"Yes." He showed them to her.

"Do you carry the keys?"

"Sure."

"Did you ever use them?"

"Yes."

"What happened?"

"I was showing my grandpa — It's a long story."

"I'd love to hear it."

"Never mind," the sheriff said, and Deputy Young snickered. The sheriff stared at the wall and said, dreamily, "Performance reviews coming up." The Deputy snickered again.

Mr. Delaney and Abby came back from the kitchen. "My client is happy to cooperate to the fullest extent with the police. Please do check her mailbox. — BUT," he said, as Sheriff Cornflower moved, "I need to be present, and you need to tell us what this is all about."

"Come on, then," the sheriff said. "Those forensic guys get paid by the hour."

Kerry stood to go with them, but Mr. Delaney waved him down. Kerry was surprised — and, from the look on his face, Mr. Delaney was surprised, too, and somewhat suspicious — that Juss hadn't jumped up to go along.

"Is my tea ready?" Juss asked, when Mr. Delaney and the police had gone.

"Oh, yes, of course."

Kerry smiled at his employer. "I don't know what we would have done without you. I've just met you, and I feel as if we've been friends for years and years. I hope I don't presume by saying so."

Juss flushed.

I wish Schatzi were here. She always knows the right thing to say.

Abby brought in a tray of napkins, teaspoons, filled cups on saucers, sugar, cream, a plate of lemon wedges for Kerry, and a plate of shortbread cookies.

"We'll have a tea party," Abby said, placing the tray, without mishap, on the coffee table. "The cookies are only storebought, but they're pretty good."

"Abby," Kerry said, "what's happened? You're taking this in stride. I'm delighted you aren't anxious, of course, but I would have expected you to be."

"I am anxious. Naturally, I am. Who wouldn't be?" Abby ran a hand over her hair, smoothing it rather than rucking it up. "But I'm not alone. I have friends."

"You always did."

Abby patted Kerry's hand, causing him to slop some of his tea into his saucer. "I know. But I believe it, now. I believe it matters." Her eyes looked a bit unfocused, as if she were thinking of something else.

The heavy footfalls of Carlton Cornflower and DW Delaney came up the stairs. *They built these old houses to last. I'm not certain a modern staircase would hold both of them at once.*

Abby opened the door before they reached it and offered refreshment again, which was again refused.

The sheriff took out his notebook and pen. So did Juss. Both wrote something on the top of a page. Sheriff Cornflower gave Juss a suspicious look; she nodded, one professional to another.

He sighed deeply and asked Abby, "Can you account for your movements today?"

Abby sank into her chair, so pale she was almost blue. "What's happened?"

"Nothing," Mr. Delaney assured her. "Nobody's been hurt. If you don't want to answer the question, I'll tell the sheriff what you told me in the kitchen and we'll go from there."

"No. No, it's all right. You scared me." She rubbed the arms of her chair; when they were younger, she had told Kerry it helped her put her thoughts in order. He could see her gaining control of the jumble the sheriff's question had provoked.

"I spent the night at Kerry's. I got up with them, had breakfast, helped Schatzi get the kids off to school and Kerry off to work."

"Schatzi is. . . ?"

"My wife," Kerry said. "Gretchen Metzenberger Dashingly."

The sheriff gave him a dirty look and Kerry spelled the name.

"All right," Sheriff Cornflower said. "About what time did everybody leave?"

"Oh . . . 7:30?"

Kerry nodded.

"And you confirm this, sir?"

"I do."

"Then what?"

Abby rubbed the arms of her chair again. "Then Schatzi — Gretchen Dashingly — sat me down and told me she and Kerry had been to Like-a-Pro, the sports shop in the mall—"

"The Blankenbaker Mall, is that correct?"

"Yes, sir. She said the salesman had told them that the two men who were witnesses in my court case—"

"This was the case Jack Pitt prosecuted? The one you gave a statement on yesterday?"

"Yes."

"Go on."

"Um. She told me the two witnesses got really mad about missing so much work. She said she and Kerry wanted me to be careful, just in case."

Mr. Dashingly and the sheriff nodded to each other and Kerry remembered that Mr. Dashingly had said he was going to call the sheriff right away.

"Mr. Dashingly, you talked to this salesman?"

"Yes, sir."

"Do you confirm that this is what you and your wife agreed to tell Miss Andrews?"

"Yes, sir."

"All right, Miss Andrews. What next?"

"Well, it was about eight, and Schatzi — Mrs. Dashingly — went into her office."

"Where is she employed?"

"Oh! I mean she went into her office at home. She designs web sites for small businesses."

"No kidding? I carve animals out of wood, and I've been thinking of — Never mind. Go on. She went into her office."

"Um. I sat there thinking about what happened to Mr. Pitt, and getting more and more afraid, and then I thought, 'I'm safe here,' and then I thought that was selfish, because maybe I *wasn't* safe there, and maybe nobody there was safe because *I* was there. I mean, we don't know who ran into Mr. Pitt or why, or if the person is in any way rational, right? I mean, *you* might know, but *I* don't know. So I thought I ought to leave and take any danger away with me. It seemed the right thing to do."

Kerry, overcome with affection for this rather rabbity woman who had forced herself out into a frightening world in order to draw a threat away from others, took her cold hand and held it.

"Did you tell Mrs. Dashingly you were leaving?"

Abby shook her head. "No, sir. I thought she would try to stop me. She's a very brave woman."

Kerry squeezed Abby's hand appreciatively.

"Your car is impounded," the sheriff said. "How did you get away?"

"I called a Thompson from my cell phone and met it on the corner." *Thompson* was what everybody in Jorisburg called a Thompson's Taxi, the only cab service in town.

"At what time?"

"Maybe nine? Yes, it was nine, because the top-of-the-hour news was on, and I know it was after eight and

188

I was home by ten, so it had to have been nine when I was in the cab."

"And how do you know you were home by ten?"

"I watched Give Me A Break. That game show that's been on for about a million years?"

"And then?"

"I got home, picked up the mail — That's how I knew the paper in the box wasn't mail, because I cleared out the mailbox when I got home from Kerry's. Um. I couldn't concentrate on anything. I watched the news, listened to the radio, read the papers. I tried to read a book. I tried to eat lunch. I couldn't think." Color rushed back into her face. "Then Alan — Deputy Cunningham — came to check on me. He said you asked him to."

"That's correct. Mr. Delaney called us and said Mr. and Mrs. Dashingly were concerned for you, and we sent Deputy Cunningham to make sure you were all right."

"And to make sure I really came home?" Abby said, rather shrewdly, Kerry thought.

The sheriff chuckled. "Yes, ma'am. That brings us to two. Then what?"

"Officer Cunningham didn't stay long but, while he was here, I got a phone call from Marsha Knowles, saying she was going to sue me for damages. She asked me to meet her at the food court at the Perfect Fit Spa at three. Deputy Cunningham looked up Mr. Delaney's number for me, but I couldn't take any more handouts. It's time I got back on my own feet. I knew I could afford Robert Byrum — he was my lawyer before — so I called and left a message for him."

Kerry released Abby's hand and sat back, slightly stunned. *Of all the times for Abby to decide to go it alone.*

189

"Did you call another Thompson?"

"Um, no. I walked to The Clunker Brothers and rented a car. That little blue Datsun in the parking space downstairs. And I drove to the spa and I went to the food court, but she never showed up. So I bought some birthday presents for my nephew and I came back here and I saw that paper in the mailbox and I called Juss, and then you showed up."

Juss said, "And I hired you and now DW is your lawyer, right?"

Abby smiled faintly. "Yes. I guess I'm not ready to stand on my own two feet yet, after all."

"Sure you are!" Juss said. "But sometimes you need somebody to stand on the other end of the rug so people can't pull it out from under you any more."

Oh, well put!

"Any witnesses?" the sheriff asked.

Bewildered, Abby asked, "To what?"

"To you being at the spa and to when you got home. Anybody there when you saw the paper in the mailbox?"

"No. Oh, I ate at the food court, and I talked to a counterman and told him I was supposed to meet Marsha Knowles at three. I don't know his name or if he'd remember, though."

"Okay, Carlton," Mr. Delaney said. "Your turn. What can you tell us?"

The sheriff flipped back in his notebook. "We got a call at 3:15 pm today from Marsha Knowles, saying she went to her vehicle to get a towel and found a piece of paper stuck under her windshield wiper, unfolded, face down so it was only readable from inside the car. She took it out and read it and called us. We called you, to see if you were all right, but your line was busy. So we came on over, and we saw a piece of paper in your mailbox and asked if we could read it. You had already called a lawyer."

"I guess that's why she stood me up. I guess she found that paper and called you, and I went right out of her mind. Was my paper the same as hers? What is it?"

"Well, Miss Andrews, the forensics guys have it, to test for fingerprints and DNA and whatever cra — clues they test for, but both of them read the same. Both of them were printed on a laser printer, very large type, like an advertising flyer. Both of them say *You're next.*"

Chapter 32

Juss sat forward, leaning across the coffee table to force eye contact with Abby, who (Juss had to admit there was no better word) goggled at the sheriff.

"No," Juss said, with a firmness she had learned from Mama D. "You are *not* next. I can't speak for Marsha Knowles, but you are not next. You are not ever."

"You can't—"

"I am not leaving this apartment without you. We've got alarms and security systems out the whatsis. You can stay with us until the cops get their—" *Oops!* "I mean, until the police solve the case."

Sheriff Cornflower consulted his notebook. "Injustice H. Chocolate," he said, not batting an eye, "1 Spadena Street of this city, correct?"

"Yes, sir."

He read her office land line number and cell phone number for her to confirm, then asked Abby, "Will you be accepting her offer? Will 1 Spadena Street be your address until further notice?"

"Say yes," Juss said.

DW said, "You might as well. I think it's a good idea. But, if you do go there, *stay* there. Don't go haring off 'investigating' things."

"I won't. Believe me, I won't."

He cocked a look at Juss, who avoided his eyes.

"All right, then." The sheriff tucked his pen and notebook away. "You'll be hearing from us."

192

"Through me," DW said.

The sheriff nodded, but Juss thought it was more goodbye than agreement, because he nodded to each of them, then left.

"I'll help Abby pack," Juss said. "How long do you think? A week?"

"A week?" Abby said. "That long?"

"Who knows?" Juss said. "You'll like it there. Doris is a great cook, and Kerry comes every day — every weekday, of course — and he and Schatzi and the kids can come visit and even have sleepovers."

As they left the room, she heard DW say, "You see how she is?" but she ignored him.

Abby stood, lost in her own bedroom.

"Suitcase?" Juss suggested.

"Suitcase," Abby repeated. "Yes. I haven't even unpacked from Kerry's." She dragged the suitcase onto her bed and snapped it open. "I should have washed my dirty clothes as soon as I got home."

"We have a washer and dryer."

Juss took in the room's clutter and had misgivings about inviting a pack-rat into her organized space. *It's only for a week. Or so. And it'll be worth it.* The misgivings fell away and she smiled what Kerry would have called a happy emu smile.

Chapter 33

"Can't you leave that old machine in the office and relax?" Doris asked.

"No rest for the wicked," Juss said, looking up from her laptop. "If I have to work, I'd rather work in here with you guys. But if it bothers you. . . ." She faked getting up.

Doris waved her down, as she had expected.

"No, no, you stay right where you are. The TV won't bother you?"

"No."

They were upstairs in the television room, all of them cozy in flannel and socks, all of them having laughed in delight when they saw the others be-flanneled.

"You two got enough medicine?" Doris asked.

Juss checked her wine glass and chocolate plate. "I'm in good shape."

"Me, too," said Abby.

Doris settled into the couch next to Abby, and Juss, in an armchair with a folding table in front of it, got back to her reading.

She was going through Marsha's blog entries on the accident. The first one was vitriolic. *Well, they're all either vitriolic or gloating or both. Unless they're self-pitying. Let's see — the prosecutor called her. Preening self-importance. Mr. Pitt. Jibber-jabber. Now he's Jack. Blah, blah, blah, now he's Jackie. Ooo, now he's Jerkie. The Jerk. Not so good.*

194

Pitt had begun the case with an appeal to Marsha's good citizenship, which had fallen on deaf ears until she had realized her insurance was going to go up and she'd have to pay for all repairs if she had caused the accident. Pitt had told her that, if it could be proved in criminal court to be Abby's (or, in Marsha's terms, Blubber Baby's) fault, she wouldn't have her premiums raised and Blubber Baby would have to pay for everything. So Marsha had cooperated, like the good citizen she was.

He had started out "flirtatious", which she had accepted as only natural. As the case dragged on, he had made stronger advances. She didn't go so far as to give a play-by-play, but she flat-out stated they were having an affair.

Do people not know *this is the Internet? Do people not* realize *anybody in the whole wide freakin' world can read this stuff? Do they not* know *the meaning of pride or discretion or privacy? I'm going to have to wash my eyes out with soap after reading this.*

It wasn't that Marsha expected Jack Pitt to divorce his wife and marry her, but she had ultra-sensitive antennae for attitudes toward herself, and she could tell he didn't view her with the respect she deserved. Even when she insisted on being treated with respect, she could tell he didn't *mean* it.

More and more of her anger included Jack Pitt, along with Abby, Judge Walkin and the witnesses. Suddenly, her anger against Pitt went nova, and she posted a white-hot rant against public officials who use their positions to take advantage of innocent women.

Subsequent "accident" entries were about the high cost of car repairs and how all mechanics were crooks.

Juss closed out the saved entries and surfed directly to Marsha's blog. *Wonder what she's posted in the past few days?*

Everything in the past week or so was fairly benign but all about Marsha: her restaurant reviews, what she was wearing to work, what she had for lunch and supper, what music she was listening to. That alone was suspicious, given the visceral nature of other posts.

She remembered wondering if Pitt had had a blog, too. Thinking about it made her feel creepy-crawly. *That's DW's job, if it turns out it needs to be done.* DW would be proud of her, not trying to preempt his work.

Her best show was coming on. She logged off and shut down the laptop, stretched, picked up her medicine and stuffed herself in between Doris and Abby.

Happy

Chapter 34

Abby was glad when Doris stood and stretched and said, "Bedtime for yours truly." It had been a long, draining day, and she would have liked to turn in sooner, but her bed was the couch.

Juss had taken her upstairs when they first got in, Mr. Delaney insisting on carrying her luggage. Juss had the entire upper floor, with her own bathroom and a kitchenette.

"Doris and I lived up here when we were taking care of Granny Ruth, toward the end," Juss told her. "Granny Ruth had the bedroom downstairs. When she passed, Doris moved down into the real house, and I stayed up here. You take my bed and I'll take the daybed."

Abby, to her surprise as much as anyone's, had finally prevailed and Juss had agreed to keep her own bed for herself.

Now, Juss collected the empty "medicine" dishes and carried them into the kitchen. They washed and dried them and put them away.

By the time that was done, Abby was asleep on her feet. She had a vague impression of Juss offering her first turn at the bathroom and of herself actually accepting, of Juss having made up the couch while she, Abby, was in the bathroom, of Juss talking and of herself answering somehow, of Juss realizing how tired she was and turning out all the lights except a nightlight to guide her to the bathroom.

~*~

The next thing she knew, it was morning.

At first, she thought she was in her apartment, with sounds of the downstairs neighbors vibrating up through the floor. Then she opened her eyes and knew where she was. She was having a sleepover with her new friend. *No, my cousin's boss. No, my new friend. I think. New friends, plural.*

She waited for the familiar twist in her stomach that came with the questions: *What if they don't like me when they get to know me? How long before they get tired of me and drop me?* Here she was, technically a grown-up, and she was still asking junior-high questions. Was that going to be forever? Did anybody else in the whole world ask junior-high questions once they escaped from the cesspit that was junior high?

The gut twist she expected didn't come. The questions didn't seem to apply. This didn't feel like that kind of friendship. For one thing, Schatzi hadn't called to reassure her. That meant that Kerry and Schatzi trusted Juss and Doris. That meant she was safe in trusting them, too.

How peculiar.

~*~

"I'll give you the fifty-cent tour," Doris said, after breakfast. "Just put the dishes in the sink."

"I'll wash them," Abby said, eager to pull her own weight.

"No, leave them. I got a girl who takes care of the dishes for me."

"Ha, ha." Juss cut another small square of fresh apple strudel.

Abby tried to keep up without getting in the way as

Doris explained the extent of cleaning she did in each room:

"Waiting room is easy — dustmop the floor and dust the chairs and tables and lamps, straighten the magazines, and lay out the newspaper. Put the newspaper in the recycling at the end of the day. Living room is more — dust everything and run the vacuum. Pick up anything lying around loose."

Abby didn't see anything out of place, except Kerry's laptop and the books he had stacked on a long side table.

"Juss' office, she takes care of. The upstairs is hers, so she takes care of that, too. I sweep up the kitchen every day, mop once a week or more often, if it needs it. Naturally, I keep the counter and sink and stove and table clean, and I clean out the refrigerator every week the day before grocery day — make sure nothing's gone over."

They don't need my help. This is charity. This is pity.

Doris pointed to a door to the right at the end of the hall. "That's my room. I take care of that." She opened the other door. "This is the utility room and the way out to the garage. Come on in and I'll show you how to work the washer and dryer. Juss said you had clothes to wash."

When Abby had joined her in the utility room, Doris closed the door and regarded her with a slight frown, her arms crossed.

Abby didn't blame her for frowning. "I'll do whatever work I'm given while I'm here," she said, "but I know I'm not really hired, and I won't accept a salary."

"Don't you tell me you won't let us help you out with Mr. Delaney. That would hurt Juss' feelings so bad."

Abby hunched her shoulders. "Anything I do is wrong. It's wrong to hurt somebody's feelings, it's rude to turn down an offer of help, and I really might need a good lawyer. If she'll let me, I'll pay her back when this is over and I'm working again. But this so-called 'job' — It's wrong to take money for nothing. It doesn't matter if you're taking it from somebody who has plenty of it, excuse me for saying so."

Doris smiled a sweet and open smile. "You think that girl is filthy rich, but you wouldn't take a cent if you could help it." She nodded approvingly. "You're good people, you and your cousins."

I think that girl is filthy rich?

Doris chuckled. "Her great-grandma Scrooge McDuck made a will leaving everything to Juss' Grannie Ruth, saying Grannie Ruth couldn't leave anything of it to Juss and Juss couldn't even live in either of the houses, here or in Highgate Commons. DW broke that living-in-the-house clause so Juss and I could take care of Grannie Ruth before she needed to go into a care home. But the judge was a pal of Old Lady Scrooge, and he wouldn't break the inheritance clause. So Grannie Ruth left everything to *me*. Then DW and I fixed it up to put it all in a trust, and all the household bills would get paid out of it and Juss and I would get allowances. She started this Life Coach business to have some extra."

"Which she spends on other people," Abby guessed.

"It's her pleasure. I don't like people who take advantage of that. I've gotten to where I can size that attitude up pretty fast. I don't see it in you or Kerry or Miss Greta."

"Schatzi."

"She never told me I could call her that."

Abby was taken aback by this nicety, one she had never encountered before. It was decidedly odd, someone who took even less for granted than she would have, and displayed the attitude as dignity rather than mousiness. *Maybe I'm not a wimp. Maybe my instincts aren't always wrong.*

"So," Doris said, "when Juss invited you to stay, I thought, 'Uh-oh. We'll see about that.' But after spending some time with you, I think the only danger is of her trying to make you into her little doll-baby and give you things you don't want to take. She can't stand to have something somebody else doesn't have. What are you going to do with a girl like that? The child was raised by hippies."

Chapter 35

Juss was lingering over a cup of coffee and a last bite of strudel when the bell rang.

"I'll get it!" she shouted.

"I know you will," Doris' voice floated in from the utility room.

It was Kerry.

"Come in, come in. Have some coffee and cake."

"No, but thank you." Kerry hung up his overcoat and took three envelopes out of his pocket. "Is Abby up yet?"

"She's in the back with Doris." Juss led the way. "How are Schatzi and the kids? And is it Schatzi's parents who live with you?"

"Next door to us, in the other half of the duplex. Mr. and Mrs. Metzenberger, Schatzi's parents, yes. Everyone's fine, thank you."

Kerry exchanged good mornings with Doris and his cousin, then handed Abby the envelopes.

"The children made these for you."

Abby opened the one with her name sprawled all over the envelope's front in spidery capitals. Inside was a daisy made of sliced almonds glued (in this case, rather randomly) onto a center made of yellow construction paper.

"Lisa, of course," Kerry said.

The second envelope was printed clearly with *Abigail Andrews* and *with love from Angela Dashingly*. The daisy in this envelope was utterly perfect.

"Joel thought what the girls did was 'baby stuff', but he didn't want you to think he didn't miss you, so he did this." Kerry handed her a third envelope, with Abby written in precise but somehow muscular cursive.

Joel had made a card out of a sheet of white paper with a painfully detailed drawing of a car on the front.

"That's my car, before the accident," Abby said, showing the drawing to Doris and Juss.

"He got out some pictures from last year, so he could get all the details right."

Inside Joel's card, he had written *Race back to see us soon! Love, Joel.*

Abby *ooed* and cooed over all of it, and put the nuts that fell off Lisa's daisy back into the envelope. "Tell them thank you so much."

Juss eyed the envelopes with wistful envy. *I wonder if I have brothers and sisters somewhere? I wonder if I have cousins who would make cute things for me, if they knew me and liked me? Aunts? Uncles? Anybody?*

She knew her father was an only child — Great-grandmama had been so grateful for that, or had said she was, in their one meeting. Granny Ruth had also been an only, and so had Great-grandmama, which didn't surprise her. She had never looked up Great-grandmama's or Granny Ruth's late husbands' families, since both men had died before she came back into the fold — or as far into the fold as Granny Ruth could bring her. She had never been able to trace her mother's people with the minimal information Doris knew about her. *Why bother, anyway?*

"I'm eager to get back to the library," Kerry said. "I'm ready to begin at the top of another column, where the older books are."

"Not on Saturday!"

"No, no, on Monday. I wanted to bring the children's cards to Abby and see how she's doing."

"I have an appointment with a client this morning," Juss said, reluctantly. For once, she would rather stay home.

"A real one," Doris asked, "or did somebody break a fingernail?"

"Let's have some respect," Juss said, although she had to agree that some people didn't know how lucky they were. Still, to be fair. . . . "Just because other people have real problems doesn't mean that a little problem isn't the biggest problem some people have. Oh, you know what I mean! Besides, this is a real one. This is that man trying to get through that divorce. He has no idea how to take care of himself, and his mother wants him to move back in with her and he doesn't want to. Why do people try to smother people? It isn't good for either of them. —What's the matter?"

She sniffed the air, but detected nothing that would cause a coughing fit in everybody else. *Must be something going around. Hope I don't catch it, too.* She pictured everybody tucked up on couches and in beds, and her, the only healthy one, bringing them all tea and chicken soup. Kerry would probably have to go home, though, but that would leave her two patients.

"Are you guys okay? Should I cancel my appointment?"

They all assured her they were fine. That was a *good* thing, naturally.

~*~

Juss spent a couple of hours with her client, coaching his life for him. She presented him with prices and schedules

204

for several levels of cleaning services, a variety of personal chefs, and websites of several mail-order cooking packages or pre-cooked meal packages.

So he was happy and Juss was happy.

She looked forward to getting home and doing her share of cleaning with Abby and Doris. *Got to remember not to do too much. She has to believe we need her. It isn't nice to make people feel like charity cases. And she isn't. She won't take simple help. Pig-headed.*

That set off a chain of jumbled thoughts, playing in the background as she headed back to Spadena Street. *Abby. Kerry's kids' cards. Abby's car. Before and after pictures. Accident. Abby's car after the accident. Abby's car in the impound lot. Abby's rental car. Marsha's loaner car—*

She jerked, inadvertently tapping the brakes and startling herself.

Marsha had found the threatening message on the windshield of her car. *Which car?* Did Car-O-Practor call her at work and say it was under the wiper of her real car, or was it under the wiper of her loaner car? If it was on her loaner car, how did the killer know which car in the spa's huge parking lot was hers? Had he, she, or they been watching her? *Her blog!* She had posted pictures of the brown Volvo on her blog, where anybody could see it. Anybody would know where she worked, and even her schedule. The witnesses worked at the mall across the road. One of them could cover for the other one while the other one ran around leaving warnings.

She pulled into a parking spot on the street so she could think without endangering her fellow motorists.

She ought to call DW. Should she? Was this important enough to bother him about? Okay, the witnesses were mad at both Marsha and Abby — as well as at Jack Pitt — according to that salesman Kerry and Schatzi talked to. Maybe not mad enough to hurt anybody, but maybe mad enough to use Pitt's death as the basis for a little practical-jokery pay-back for the lost work time. That made sense. Not very important, then. Maybe.

She should at least leave a message on DW's office machine, but not call his cell phone for something that might not even be important.

"Hi, this is Juss Chocolate. I'm heading over to the Car-O-Practor, where Marsha has her car in for repair. It occurred to me to wonder if that threat was left on the Miata or on her loaner car. If it was on the Miata, somebody at the body shop would have had to call her and tell her — and, come to think of it, whoever did it would have to know where she took her car for repair. Oh, but that was in the trial transcript, when she presented the estimate as evidence of the damage. Anyway, I'm going to drop in on my way home and see if they can tell me if anybody found something on Marsha's Miata and called her at work. While I'm at it, if they haven't done her car yet, I'll snap some pictures of the damage before it's repaired so if Marsha *does* take Abby to court for damages, there's no way she can claim for more than there is. Well, I guess that's all. 'Bye."

~*~

The red Miata sat gleaming in the dappled sunlight. It was a funny color: bright red in the sunny patches and almost black in the shady ones.

Is it out here because they're finished with it, or because they haven't started yet? Juss parked behind it, got out and walked around to the front. *Haven't started yet. Happy! Right headlight smashed, front bumper all bunged up. Need to get some shots of that. If it really is Marsha's. Better make sure, before I waste time.*

Inside the shop, an older man in Car-O-Practor coveralls rubbed his hands with a stained cloth while he regarded the underside of an elevated work in progress.

Juss stood at the open door and waved. "Yoo-hoo! Hi. This is Marsha's car, isn't it? Marsha Knowles?"

"That black-cherry red Miata. Yeah. Friend of hers?"

"I don't know her real well. She seems nice."

He shrugged. "She don't like waiting. Washed the car before she brung it in, I'll say that much. Not many do that."

The man's nametag said "Mason". She made a mental note, in case the police needed his testimony.

"Marsha said there was something on her windshield yesterday. Did she mean this windshield, or the one on her loaner car?"

"I don't know, lady."

"If it was this car, wouldn't somebody here have found it and called her?"

"Yeah. That makes sense. It must have been the other one, then. I was on all day yesterday, and I never seen anything stuck on the car. We kind of keep an eye on them, you know."

"That's what I figured. Thanks."

Returning to the Miata, she pulled out her phone and snapped pictures of any damage she could spot, sending them to DW's inbox.

"Do you mind?" A hard nasal voice tapped out the syllables.

Juss slipped the phone into her jacket pocket. A petite young woman with a salon tan, red lacquered nails, and expensive black hair glared at her.

207

Marsha Knowles!

"Gosh," Juss said. "Do I mind what?"

"What are you doing to my car?"

"Nothing." Juss tried out what Doris called her sweet innocent Bambi face. "Just looking at it. It's nice."

Marsha's eyes narrowed. "I heard you ask about me. Who are you?"

She thinks I left the threat! Oh my gosh, that's all I need — to call DW from jail. He'd love that!

Think fast! Think fast! "I'm Esther Pressler. Maybe you've read my blog? I've read yours."

"Oh, have you? Well, I've never heard of you. And I find it a bit intrusive, approaching me personally."

I didn't approach you, Miss Rude, I approached your car. And if you don't want people intruding on you, you've got a weird way of showing it, posting it on the Internet every time you blow your nose. "I'm sorry," she said. "I didn't mean to. I pulled in to check the place out because you'd recommended them, and I recognized your car from the blog. I got a kick out of that. I'd better go."

Marsha stepped into her path. "What are you up to?"

"I'm not up to anything! I happened to stop in and I recognized your car. That's all there is to it."

Smiling, Marsha said, "A fan girl? Really?"

Juss almost choked on it, but said, "Yeah, you got me."

"I'll tell you what: There's a great little coffee shop down the street. Why don't we go there and talk about things? I'd like to know more about you, too. Come on."

DW is gonna kill me! "No, I really need to—"

208

The smile hardened. "Why not? What's the matter?"

Sorry, DW. "I'd love to come. Let me get my purse. It's in my car."

"My treat." Marsha wrapped a red-nailed hand around Juss' upper arm. Juss tried to disengage, but the nails tightened.

Has this woman never heard of personal space? Judging from the way she drives and the way she blogs, apparently not. Juss wondered what they were going to talk about— *No, I know what we're going to talk about. We're going to talk about Marsha. I am going to hear a whole lot more than I ever wanted to know about Marsha Knowles.*

"Now," Marsha said, when they were off the lot. "What were you doing, poking around my car? You seemed to be inspecting it pretty closely, especially the front. What were you looking for?"

"The front is really cool. It looks like a little face. Don't you think it looks like a little face?"

"I never thought about it. A face on the front of my car."

"Plus, I read about the accident on your blog and saw the pictures you posted."

Marsha froze, jerking Juss to a halt. "The pictures I posted."

"Of the damage from the accident. It still makes me mad that that awful woman got off Scot-free. That wasn't right."

"No," Marsha said. "It wasn't."

Halfway down the block, Marsha turned left, into an alley. Juss tried to resist, but those long red nails bit into her arm even through her jacket.

"I don't want to go in there," Juss said. "It smells."

"It's a shortcut."

Juss pulled back. "I don't like alleys."

"Too damn bad." Marsha got behind her and pushed. "I don't like nosy people."

"I explained!"

"I think you lied, bitch!"

Okay, this has gone far enough. I don't care if it's privileged information. I don't care if I get in trouble with DW. "It wasn't me! I didn't have anything to do with that paper!"

"What paper?"

"The one you found on your car."

Marsha shoved her up against a brick wall, deep in the shadows.

Juss' surprised "Uff!" didn't mask the clatter on the cobbles.

Both women looked down at the phone, camera app still open.

"That's mine," Juss said. *Duh! Whose else would it be?*

Marsha picked up the phone and flipped through the shots. "You were taking pictures of my car." She threw the phone into a nearby dumpster and regarded Juss with a face like sandstone.

A certainty crawled across Juss' consciousness and dug itself in. Before and after pictures. Before Jack Pitt was killed by a hit-and-run driver and after he was killed by a hit-and-run driver. A "mostly black" car in the CT 'Scape's shady parking lot. Every hair on her body stood up. *This is not happy!*

"I wanted a picture of your car," Juss said. "Fan Girl, remember?"

"Shut up!" Marsha snarled. "What did you see? What do you know?"

"Now, look. Okay," Juss said, in as calm a voice as she could manage. "You made your point. I shouldn't have been stalking you, even if you are super-cool. It was creepy. I'm sorry."

"Did you see me leave that letter?"

"Where?"

"In that shrinking violet's letterbox. Were you following me?"

DW is gonna be SO MAD!

"I said I was sorry. I know you would never do anything wrong. You know me — Fan Girl. I want to know about *you*."

"You *have* been following me! Did you see me at the coffee house?"

"What coffee house?"

Marsha clenched and unclenched her fists for five long beats. Then she said, "You saw me, didn't you? You know my routine. You had to know I work out first thing in the morning, before any of our stupid clients come in, *moaning* about how *hard* it is to stay in shape. You were following me. I could have sworn there was no other car in sight. I could have sworn it."

"I didn't see a thing."

"You must have turned the corner just as I hit him. You must have pulled over and watched me climb through the broken window. You must have seen me come out with his stupid hair."

No, no, no, no, no!

"I didn't see a thing! And if I did, I wouldn't say anything. I'm you're biggest fan! Let's have that coffee, now, okay?"

She brushed past the smaller woman, but she had only

taken two steps before Marsha grabbed her elbow and spun her around. A hard little fist caught her under the eye and knocked her against the dumpster.

"Ow! Geez!" She bounced off the metal. "What was that for?"

"That was for lying."

Now what? Okay, now I do *lie, Miss Fisticuffs.* "What if I *did* see you? He had it coming, didn't he?"

"Of course! I wouldn't do such a thing to an innocent person. Tell me — you read my blog; did you read his?"

"Ewww, as if."

Marsha laughed. "It was sleazy, all right. He thought I didn't know about it. And I didn't, at first. Then I found it, and. . . . It was about me."

I would have thought you'd love *that.*

"It was about . . . private things. He posted pictures. He posted videos. With sound."

I do not want to be hearing this.

"When I told him he had to take those entries down, he said he wouldn't. And then he lost the case! He promised me he'd see to it my car got repaired at no cost to me and that my insurance wouldn't go up, and then he *lost!* And I started getting hits on my blog from people who had read *his!*"

Juss sidled away as quickly as she dared. There was a street in either direction, with traffic and shops and people. She turned to run.

Marsha clutched a handful of curls and jerked.

"Ow! That hurts! Help! In the alley! Help me!"

Marsha spun her around and popped her again.

"Ow! Quit it!" Juss raised an arm to protect her face. When no more blows came, she peeked, and

212

saw Marsha outlined by the light at the alley's mouth, raising a length of pipe. She backed up and banged into the dumpster again. This could not be happening! *"No! Help!"*

"Shut *up*, bitch!"

"I don't think so! *HAAALP!*" Juss tried backing in another direction, came up against a drift of debris and went over backward, legs flying, breath knocked out of her. By sheer luck, her head landed on something soft. Something that squealed and scuttered deeper into the alley.

Even breathless and on her back, her body tried to run from Mr. Squeak. One flailing foot clipped her attacker's knee.

Marsha's leg buckled and she almost pitched over, the pipe flying out of her hand. While she went after it, Juss lay helpless, gasping for breath, listening to the sweet sad sound of police sirens in the distance.

Relax. Breathe. Relax. Breathe.

She heard Marsha cursing, then the clink and clunk of metal. Marsha had found her weapon of choice. Juss levered herself up and staggered in a circle, desperate to get away.

The street they'd supposedly been heading for was closer, but Marsha was between her and that avenue of escape. She took off, away from Marsha and her pipe.

"Come back here!" Marsha shouted.

Yeah, right!

The light was suddenly cut off.

Oh, God, is that a truck? Don't let them be backing in! Don't let them be blocking the way! Being bludgeoned to death within sight of safety was bitter and terribly, terribly possible. Maybe she could squeeze through. There was light on either side. It wasn't blocking the way entirely.

The "truck" grabbed her and pulled her into the blinding sunlight.

Sheriff Cornflower and Jean Louise Young plunged into the darkness.

"Stop where you are!" the sheriff shouted. "Stop!" A shot rang out nearby, and her confusion resolved itself and she knew the "truck" was DW and she was safe.

Chapter 36

A week had passed since the attack, but Juss' bruises were still vivid. Kerry had never seen an emu with two black eyes, but now he knew what one would look like.

"I'm impressed," DW said, regarding Juss with fascination. He wasn't talking about her detecting abilities.

Kerry and Schatzi sat side-by-side on a loveseat in the downstairs living room.

Doris entered with a tray of Juss' oatmeal/raisin/walnut cookies to go with the coffee they already had. She passed them out and sat on the couch with DW.

Abby scurried in with a mug for Juss. She had moved back into her apartment, but had turned out to be an excellent secretary and receptionist. Doris had limited her to that, on the grounds that Juss was capable of doing her own share of the cleaning. "Here's your refill," Abby said, handing the mug over carefully. "Fresh pot."

Juss sniffed the hazelnut brew. "Is this decaf?"

In a tiny voice, Abby said, "We're out of decaf."

"Good. Thank you."

Abby sat between DW and Doris and looked at Juss with pained sympathy. "I am still so sorry this happened to you because of me."

"It didn't happen because of you," DW said. "It happened because of *her*." He shook his head at Juss. "Didn't I tell you to stay out of police business?"

"I didn't know it was police business, I told you! I thought I was taking pictures for a civil suit and the next thing I know, that whack-job foul-mouthed hell-cat was beating my brains out."

"You gave as good as you got," Kerry said, loyally.

Juss lowered her coffee and gave him a dirty look. "I most certainly did not."

"She had a knee the size of a football."

"Hel-looo? That was an *accident*? I was *raised* by *hippies*. I don't hurt people."

DW grunted. "Lucky for you, Carlton Cornflower doesn't have the same scruples." He sat forward. "Now look: Carlton wants to be sure you stay out of and away from any future investigations you may get wind of."

"Like I'm some kind of meddler!" Juss protested, and wondered why nobody would meet her eye.

"Be that as it may," DW said, "it will astound you to know that the police were not baffled. In fact — and I hate to be the one to break this to you, but — as soon as they found Jack Pitt's broken and glass-cut body they not only realized that he was dead, but recognized the possibility that someone had killed him, and even that the person who killed him might have been someone who didn't like him very much. The police deduced that all by themselves. Isn't that amazing?"

Juss picked up a cookie and nibbled at it with an unconvincing affectation of deafness to DW's ponderous sarcasm.

"One of the names pretty far down their list was yours, Abby. As Juss found out while she wasn't meddling, the list was long and the net was wide. But they had some things to look for: A car doesn't hit a body as hard as Pitt was hit

216

without sustaining some damage. A truck, maybe, but not a car. And, somebody took a souvenir, and the most likely person to do that was the killer."

"His ponytail," Abby said. "I was right, wasn't I? I guessed it was his ponytail, once I thought about it. Marsha killed him and cut it off and planted it in my car to make it look like I killed him. And I'm the one who called police attention to it!"

"That was a *good* thing," DW said. "But they had already had their attention directed to you. A woman called and left an anonymous tip that they should look in Abigail Andrews' car if they wanted to know who killed Jack Pitt."

"Oh!" Abby raised a hand to her mouth, but the hand turned to a fist and the O of panic turned to an angry grimace.

DW said, "And that was a good thing, too." He turned a deceptively gentle look on Juss as he said, "Believe it or not, the police suspected a frame — or a prank call. They were debating whether or not to follow up when Deputy Cunningham called them. His report of your reaction when you opened that car door set the seal on their suspicion — of somebody else, not of you."

Kerry took Schatzi's hand as Abby blushed at the mention of Alan Cunningham's name.

Juss, a fragment of chocolate chip stuck in the corner of her mouth, said, "Marsha might not have started out thinking about a frame. She might have taken the ponytail for a trophy, but then she probably thought she'd better get rid of it. She saw your car at the CT 'Scape — you said in the court transcript that you go there a lot — and she stopped and planted it."

"But my car was locked! Probably. And I didn't hear the door screek."

Juss licked the chocolate off and said, "You have cardboard taped across where the window ought to be. Easy to peel off, easy to stick back on."

"Good job, Sherlock," Delaney said. "Guess what? The police got that, too. They took Abby's car and went over it immediately and thoroughly. Guess where they found fingerprints that Marsha's match? On and around the duct tape and the window. Guess where they found signs of Abby's car having hit a body? Nowhere. Guess where they found residue of the crime scene inside or outside of Abby's car? Nowhere."

Juss said, "Marsha put her car in for repair. Lucky they couldn't fix it before the police got onto her."

Kerry took another cookie. "They would have had those pictures you took, though. And they wouldn't have gotten there in time if you hadn't called DW and sent the pictures to him."

DW sighed mournfully. "Another bubble that I must pop. As soon as the police knew that the anonymous tip about Abby was a frame, they made a list of people who knew both Pitt and Abby." To Juss, he said, "They stole that idea from you."

"I hate it when you do that."

"Marsha looked good on that list, so they went to work on a search warrant for her car. They also read her blog, and they read Pitt's blog. You see, Sherlock, the police, being a part of the Criminal Justice System of our fair city — as was the victim, by the way — and being — how shall I put it? — *the police*, were able to find out about and locate and access materials you didn't even know about."

"I knew Marsha and Pitt had blogs," she muttered. "I knew that."

"Meanwhile, they called the Car-O-Practor and asked if she'd brought the car in to be repaired yet. When they said she hadn't, they asked to be notified if she did. Now that they've gone over her car, they've found evidence that her automatic car wash missed, inside and out. And, yes, her mechanic — the owner, naturally; only the best for Marsha — spotted differences in the damage between his estimate after the accident and when she brought it in to be fixed. He wasn't about to touch it until the police had seen it."

Juss passed the cookie plate around, offering it to Delaney with an *I'm such a lady, I even offer this to you* air.

DW continued, "Marsha wanted a rush job on her car. She was there in the office pushing for it when you showed up. As soon as she went out to see what you were doing, prowling around her car in broad daylight, the owner called the police, and the police called my cell phone."

His hands trembled, and his cup rattled as he lowered it to the table. Juss suddenly remembered that he had run into the alley after her *ahead* of the police, and her sullen resentment melted.

"You are one lucky crazy person," DW said. "If you didn't have such a loud mouth, we might not have found you in time."

Juss sighed. "So I got these shiners and bumps and bruises — and, possibly, rat cooties — for nothing."

"That's about the size of it." DW checked his watch and stood, brushing crumbs from his vest. "I can see myself out. Thanks for the coffee and cookies." He pointed to Juss. "You stay out of trouble from now on, yes?"

"Yes. Of course I will."

"Why do I feel as if the next line should be *But Curious George knew what to do*?"

When the door closed behind DW, Abby said, "Well, I think Juss was brilliant."

Doris said, "Thank you for pouring gasoline on that fire." She stood up. "Come on, Miss Marple, let's do these dishes and get to work."

About the Author

Marian Allen was born in Louisville, Kentucky and now lives in rural Indiana. For as long as she can remember, she's loved telling and being told stories. When, at the age of about six, she was informed that somebody got paid for writing all those books and movies and television shows, she abandoned her previous ambition (beachcomber), and became a writer.

She's worked as a high school teacher, an executive secretary, a soda jerk, a bank clerk, an accountant, and in Red Cross Youth Services.

She likes connecting and reconnecting with people, meeting new friends and keeping in touch with the friends she already has.

Her writing reflects her love of network. In her books and stories, no one exists in total isolation, but in a web of connections to family, friends, colleagues, self at former stages of maturity, perceptions, and self-images. Most of her work is fantasy, science fiction and/or mystery, though she writes horror, humor, romance, mainstream, or anything else that suits the story and characters.

Professionally, she's a member of Southern Indiana Writers.

If you enjoyed this book, please consider buying other titles by this author. Excerpts, blog posts, free stories, and buy links to various formats are available at:

Marian Allen - Fantasies, mysteries, comedies, recipes
http://MarianAllen.com